MARGARET MILLAR (1915–1994) was the author of 27 books and a masterful purveyor of psychological mysteries and thrillers. Born in Kitchener, Ontario, she spent most of her life in Santa Barbara, California, with her husband Ken Millar, who is better known by his nom de plume of Ross Macdonald. Her 1956 novel *Beast in View* won the Edgar Allan Poe Award for Best Novel. In 1965 Millar was the recipient of the *Los Angeles Times* Woman of the Year Award and in 1983 the Mystery Writers of America gave her the Grand Master Award for Lifetime Achievement. Millar's cutting wit and superb plotting have left her an enduring legacy as one of the most important crime writers of both her own and subsequent generations. *Vanish in an Instant* and *Stranger in My Grave* are also available from Pushkin Vertigo.

PRAISE FOR MARGARET MILLAR AND HER WORK

"In the whole of crime fiction's distinguished sisterhood, there is no one quite like Margaret Millar"

GUARDIAN

"One of the most original and vital voices in all of American crime fiction"

LAURA LIPPMAN, AUTHOR OF *SUNBURN*

"She has few peers, and no superior in the art of bamboozlement"

JULIAN SYMONS, *THE COLOUR OF MURDER*

"Mrs Millar doesn't attract fans, she creates addicts"

DILYS WINN

"She writes minor classics"

WASHINGTON POST

"Very original"

AGATHA CHRISTIE

The Listening Walls

PUSHKIN VERTIGO

MARGARET MILLAR

Pushkin Press
71–75 Shelton Street
London WC2H 9JQ

The Listening Walls © 1959 The Margaret Millar
Charitable Remainder Unitrust, u/a 4/12/82

First published by Random House in New York, 1959
First published by Pushkin Press in 2019

1 3 5 7 9 8 6 4 2

ISBN 13: 978-1-78227-575-6

Designed and typeset by Tetragon, London
Printed and bound by CPI Group (UK) Ltd, Croydon CRO 4YY

www.pushkinpress.com

TO VERA COOPER,
WOMAN OF
LETTERS

From her resting place in the broom closet Consuela could hear the two American ladies in 404 arguing. The closet was as narrow as the road to heaven and smelled of furniture polish and chlorine, and of Consuela herself. But it was not physical discomfort that disturbed her siesta; it was the strain of trying to understand what the Americans were arguing about. Money? Love? What else was there, Consuela wondered, and wiped the sweat off her forehead and neck with one of the clean towels she was supposed to place in the bathrooms at exactly six o'clock.

It was now seven. She refolded the towel and put it back on the pile. The manager might be a little crazy on the subject of clean towels and exact times, but Consuela was not. A few germs never hurt anybody, especially if no one knew they were there, and what was an hour, one way or the other, in the face of eternity?

Every month the manager, Señor Escamillo, herded the members of the housekeeping staff into one of the banquet rooms, yapping at their heels like a nervous terrier.

"Now hear this. I have had complaints. Yes, *complaints*. So once again we are here, and once again I say to you the Americans are our most valuable customers. We must keep them so. We must speak always American; we must think American. Now. What do the Americans hate the most passionately? Germs. So we do not give them germs. We give them clean towels. Twice a day, clean towels absolutely without germs. Now, the water. They will ask questions about the water and you will say this water from the tap is the purest water in all of Mexico City. Now. Any questions?"

Consuela had a number of questions, such as why did the manager use bottled water in his office, but self-preservation kept her silent. She needed the job. Her boyfriend had a bent for picking the wrong horses at the Hipódromo, the wrong numbers in the lottery, the wrong jai alai player in the *quiniela*.

The argument between the two ladies was continuing. Were they arguing about love? Not very likely, Consuela decided. Pedro, the elevator operator and chief spy of the establishment, addressed each of the American ladies as señora, so presumably they had husbands somewhere and were in the city on vacation.

Money? Not likely, either. Both of the ladies looked prosperous. The taller one (Wilma, her friend called her) had a genuine full-length mink coat which she wore constantly, even going down to breakfast; and when she moved along the corridor she clanked like a trolley car she had on so many bracelets. She left nothing behind in her room except a locked suitcase. Consuela had, as a matter of routine, searched through the bureau drawers, and they were all as empty as a sinner's heart. The locked suitcase and the empty drawers were naturally a great disappointment to Consuela, who had refurbished her wardrobe considerably during the months she'd worked at the hotel. Taking the odd garment here and there was not actually stealing. It was more a matter of common sense, even of justice. If some people were very rich and others very poor, things had to be evened up a bit, and Consuela was doing her part.

"Everything locked," Consuela muttered among the brooms. "And all those bracelets. Clank, clank, clank."

She picked four bath towels off the top of the pile, swung them over her left shoulder and stepped out into the hall, a handsome young woman with a haughty tilt to her head. Her confident stride and the casual way she wore the towels made her look like an athlete headed for the showers after a good day on the court or in the field.

Outside 404 she paused a moment to listen, but all anyone could hear, even with ears of a fox, was the roar of traffic from the *avenida* below. Everyone in the city seemed to be going somewhere, and Consuela had an urge to run down the back stairs and go with them. Her feet, large and flat in their straw *espadrilles*, ached to be running. But instead they stood quietly outside 404 until the tall one, Wilma, opened the door.

She was dressed to go out to dinner in a red silk suit. Every curl, every ring, every bracelet was in place, but only half her make-up had been applied, so that one eye was dull and pale as a fish's and the other sparkled with a gold lid and a bright black fringe under a gaily improbable arch. When the paint job was completed she would be, Consuela had to admit, imposing, the kind of woman who would not have to catch the eye of a waiter because his eye would be already on her.

But she is not hembra, Consuela thought. *She has no more bosoms than a bull. Let her keep her underwear locked up. It wouldn't fit me anyway.* And Consuela, who was conspicuously *hembra*, if not downright fat, inflated her chest and rhumbaed her hips through the doorway.

"Oh, it's you," Wilma said. "Again." She turned her back with abrupt annoyance and addressed her companion. "It seems to me every time I take a breath in this place someone's pussyfooting around turning down beds or changing towels. We get about as much privacy as in a hospital ward."

Amy Kellogg, standing by the window, made a sound of embarrassed protest, a kind of combination of *ssshh* and *oh dear.* The sound was Amy's own, the resonance of her personality, and an expert could have detected in it the echoes of all the things she hadn't had the nerve to say in her lifetime, to her parents, her brother Gill, her husband Rupert, her old friend Wilma. She was not, as her brother Gill frequently pointed out, getting any younger. It was time for her to take a firm stand, be decisive and businesslike. *Don't let people walk all over you,* he often said, while his own boots went tramp, crunch, grind. *Make your own decisions,* he said, but every time she did make a decision it was taken away from her and cast aside or improved, as if it were a toy a child had made, crude and grotesque.

Wilma said, giving herself another golden eyelid, "I feel as if someone's spying on me."

"They're only trying to provide good service."

"The towels she put in this morning stank."

"I didn't notice."

"You smoke. Your sense of smell has deteriorated. Mine hasn't. They stank."

"I wish you wouldn't—do you think you ought to talk like this in front of the girl?"

"She doesn't understand."

"But the travel agency said everyone on the hotel staff spoke English."

"The travel agency is in San Francisco. We're here." Wilma made *here* sound like a synonym for *hell.* "If she can speak English why doesn't she say something?"

Wouldn't you like to know, Consuela thought, swishing cold water nonchalantly around the washbasin. She not speak English, ha! She, who had once lived in Los Angeles, until the immigration authorities had caught up with her father and sent the whole family back with a busload of wetbacks; she, who had a genuine American boyfriend and was the envy of the whole neighborhood because she would one day, with the cooperation of the right

12

horses, numbers and jai alai players, return to Los Angeles and walk among the movie stars. Not speak English! *Ho ho to you, Wilma, with no more bosoms than a bull!*

"She's really very pretty," Amy said. "Don't you think so?"

"I hadn't noticed."

"She is. Terribly pretty," Amy repeated, watching Consuela's reflection in the bathroom mirror for some sign that the girl had understood, a blush, a brightening of the eye. But Consuela was an older hand at pretense than Amy was at exposing pretenses. She came out of the bathroom, smiling, bland, and turned down each of the twin beds and plumped up the pillows. For Consuela the pretense was like a game. It could be a dangerous one, if the Americans complained to the manager, who knew she could speak English perfectly. But she couldn't resist it any more than she could resist pilfering a pretty nylon slip, a gaudy belt, or a pair of lace panties.

Amy, who knew a little about games too, said, "What's your name? Do you speak English?"

Consuela grinned and shrugged and spread her hands. Then she turned so quickly that her *espadrilles* squeaked in protest, and a moment later she was speeding down the hall to her broom closet. The grin had dropped off her face, and her throat felt tight as a cork in a bottle. In the narrow darkness, without quite knowing why, she crossed herself.

"I don't trust that girl," Wilma said.

"We could move to another hotel."

"They're all the same. The whole country's the same. Corrupt."

"We've only been here two days. Don't you think…"

"'I don't have to think. I can smell. Corruption always smells."

Wilma sounded positive, as she always did when she was wrong or unsure of herself. She finished her make-up job by applying

13

a dot of lipstick to the inside corner of each eye while Amy watched, hoping that Wilma's "nerves" were not going to erupt again. The signs were all there, like the first wisps of smoke over a volcano; the trembling hands, the hard, fast breathing, the quick suspicions.

Wilma had had a bad year, a divorce (her second), the death of her parents in a plane wreck, a bout of pneumonia. She had planned the holiday in Mexico to get away from it all. Instead, she had taken it all with her. *Including,* Amy thought grimly, *me. Well, I needn't have come. Rupert said I was making a mistake and Gill called me an imbecile. But Wilma has no one left but me.*

Wilma turned away from the bureau mirror. "I look like a hag."

The wisps of smoke were becoming clouds.

"No, you don't," Amy said. "And I'm sorry I called you a poor sport. I mean…"

"This suit hangs on me like a tent."

"It's a beautiful suit."

"Of course it's a beautiful suit. It's a fine suit. It's the hag inside that's ruining it."

"Don't talk like that. You're only thirty-three."

"Only! I've lost so much weight. I'm like a stick." Wilma sat down abruptly on the edge of one of the beds. "I feel sick."

"Where? Is it your head again?"

"My stomach. Oh, God. It's like—like being poisoned."

"Poisoned? Now, Wilma, you mustn't *think* like that."

"I know. I *know.* But I feel so sick." She rolled over sideways across the bed, her hands clutching her stomach.

"I'm going to call a doctor."

"No, no—I don't trust—foreigners…"

"I can't sit here and watch you suffer."

"Oh God. I'm dying—I can't breathe…"

Her groans reached the broom closet, and Consuela pressed against the listening wall, as still and alert as a lizard on a sunny rock.

A doctor arrived before eight, a small, jaunty man with a red camellia in his buttonhole. He seemed to know what to expect; his examination was perfunctory, his questions brief. He gave Wilma a small red capsule and a teaspoon of a viscous peach-colored liquid, the remains of which he left on the bureau for future administration.

Afterward, he talked to Amy in the sitting room adjoining the bedroom. "Your friend, Mrs. Wyatt, is very high-strung."

"Yes, I know."

"She claims to have been poisoned."

"Oh, that's simply her nerves."

"I think not."

"No one would want to poison poor Wilma."

"No? Well, that's not for me to say." The doctor smiled. He had friendly eyes, the sheen and color of horehound. "But she has, in effect, been poisoned. Her malady is very common among visitors—*turista*, it is called, among other less reputable names."

"The water…?"

"That, yes, but also the change of diet, injudicious eating, the altitude. The medicine I left for her is a new antibiotic which should take care of her digestive problems. The altitude is a different matter. Even to please the tourist trade, we cannot alter it. So here you are at approximately 7400 feet when you are accustomed to sea level. San Francisco, I believe you said?"

"Yes."

"It is particularly hard on your friend because she is suffering from high blood pressure. Such people are inclined to be overactive by nature, and at this altitude overactivity can be most unwise. Mrs. Wyatt must be more cautious. Impress that on her."

Amy did not point out that nobody had been able to impress anything on Wilma for years; but she sighed, and the doctor seemed to understand.

"Explain a little, anyway," he said. "My countrymen do not take their siestas out of sheer laziness, as the comic strips would have you believe. The siesta is a sensible health precaution under our circumstances of living. You must so advise your friend."

"Wilma doesn't like to lie down in the daytime. She says it's procrastination."

"And so it is. A little procrastination is exactly what she requires."

"Well, I'll do my best," Amy said, sounding as if her best would be only a slight improvement over her worst. In fact, it seemed to Amy that the two sometimes got mixed up, and her best turned out disastrous and her worst not so bad.

The doctor's eyes moved back and forth across her face as if they were reading lines. "There's another possibility," he said, "if you're not pressed for time."

"What is it?"

"You might go down to Cuernavaca for a few days and give your friend a chance to acclimatize more gradually."

"How do you spell that?"

He spelled it and she wrote it down on a little steel-backed pad with a magnetized pen attached. Rupert had given her the set because she couldn't keep track of pens and was always having to write notes with an eyebrow pencil or even a lipstick. The lipstick ones were necessarily abbreviated. R: G.G.w.M B'k s'n. A. Only Rupert could have deciphered this to mean that Amy had taken the Scottie, Mack, to Golden Gate Park for a run and would be back soon.

"Cuernavaca," the doctor said, "is only about an hour's drive, but it's some three thousand feet closer to sea level. Pretty town, lovely climate."

"I'll tell Mrs. Wyatt about it when she wakes up."

"Which probably won't be until tomorrow morning."

"She hasn't had any dinner."

"I don't think she'll miss it," the doctor said with a dry little smile. "You, on the other hand, look as if you need something to eat."

It seemed heartless to admit to hunger with Wilma ill, so Amy shook her head. "Oh, I'm not really hungry."

"The dining room remains open until midnight. Avoid raw fruit and vegetables. A steak would be good, no condiments. A Scotch and soda, but no fancy cocktails."

"I can't very well leave Wilma."

"Why not?"

"Suppose she wakes up and needs help."

"She won't wake up." The doctor picked up his medical bag, stepped briskly to the door, and opened it. "Good night, Mrs. Kellogg."

"I—we haven't paid you."

"My charges will be added to your hotel bill."

"Oh. Well, thank you very much, Dr...?"

"Lopez." He presented his card with a neat little bow and closed the door behind him loudly and firmly as if to prove his point that Wilma wouldn't wake up.

The card read, Dr. Ernest Lopez, Paseo Reforma, 510, Tel. 11-24-14.

He left behind him a faint smell of disinfectant. While he'd been in the room the smell had been rather reassuring to Amy: germs were being killed, viruses were falling by the wayside, bad little bugs were breathing their last. But without the doctor's presence, the smell became disturbing, as if it had been put there to cover up older, subtler smells of decay, like spices on rotten meat.

Amy crossed the room and opened the grilled door of the balcony. The sound from the *avenida* was deafening, as if everyone in the city, fresh and rested after a siesta, had suddenly erupted with excitement and noise. It had rained, briefly but heavily, during the late afternoon. The streets were still glistening and the air was thin and crisp and pure. It seemed to Amy like very healthful air, until she remembered Wilma's high blood pressure. Then she closed the door again quickly, as if she half believed that the room was pressurized and she could shut out the altitude with a pane of glass and some iron grilling.

"Poor Wilma," she said aloud, but the sound didn't emerge the way she intended it to. It came out, tight and small, from between clenched teeth.

She heard her own voice betraying her friendship, and she walked away from it with guilty haste, toward the bedroom.

Wilma was asleep, still wearing her red silk suit, and her bracelets, and her golden eyelids. She looked dead enough to bury.

Amy switched off the lamp and went back to the living room. It was eight o'clock. Across the *avenida* a church bell began to toll, striving to be heard above the clang of trolley cars and the horns of taxis. Back home it was only six o'clock, Amy thought. Rupert would still be working in the garden, with Mack nearby stalking butterflies and Jerusalem crickets, and letting them go, of course, if he caught any, because Scotties were very civilized dogs. Or, if the fog had moved in from the bay, the two of them would be inside, Rupert reading the Saturday papers in the den, with Mack perched on the back of his chair looking gloomily over Rupert's shoulder as if he took a very dim view of what was going on in the world.

The big man and the little dog seemed so vivid, so close, that when the knock came on the door she jumped in shock at the intrusion on her private world.

She opened the door, expecting only the girl with the towels again. But it was an elderly Mexican man carrying an object loosely wrapped in newspaper.

"Here is the box the señora ordered this afternoon."

"I didn't order any box."

"The other señora. She wished it initialed. I bring it in person, not trusting my no-good son-in-law." He removed the newspaper carefully as if he were unveiling a statue. "It is a beautiful box. Everyone agrees?"

"It's lovely," Amy said.

"The purest silver. None purer. Feel how heavy."

He handed her the hammered silver box. She almost dropped it, its weight was so unexpected in spite of his warning.

He grinned with delight. "You see? The purest of silver. The señora said it looks like the sea. I have never see the sea. I make a box that looks like the sea and I have never see the sea. How is it possible?"

"Mrs. Wyatt—the señora is asleep right now. I'll give it to her when she wakes up." Amy hesitated. "The box is paid for?"

"The box, yes. My services, no. I am an old man. I run like lightning through the streets, not trusting my no-good son-in-law. I run all the way here so the señora would have her beautiful box tonight. She said, 'Señor, this box is of such beauty I cannot bear to be without it for one night.'"

It was practically the last thing on earth Wilma would have said but Amy was in no mood to argue.

"For the señoras," he added righteously, "I run anywhere. Even though I am an old man I run."

"Would four pes—"

"A very old man. With much family trouble and a bad kidney."

In spite of his age and infirmity and running through the streets he seemed ready to talk at considerable length. She gave him six pesos, knowing it was too much, just to get rid of him.

She put the box on the coffee table, wondering why Wilma, who always made such a fuss about being charged for extraweight baggage on planes, should have bought so heavy an object, and for whom it was intended. Probably for herself, Amy thought. Wilma rarely squandered money on other people unless she was in an elated mood, and God knew there was no evidence of that on this trip.

She opened the box. The initials were on the inside of the lid, engraved so elaborately that she had difficulty deciphering them. R.J.K.

"R.J.K." She repeated the letters aloud as if to clarify them and to conjure up an image to match them. But the only R.J.K. she could think of was Rupert, and it didn't seem likely that Wilma would buy so expensive a gift for Rupert. Most of the time Amy's husband and her best friend were barely civil to each other.

3

It was Sunday afternoon when Wilma awoke from her long sleep. She felt weak and hungry, but her mind was extraordinarily clear, as if a storm had passed through her during the night leaving the inner air fresh and clean.

As she showered and dressed, it seemed to her for the first time in many years that life was very simple and logical. She wished there were somebody around to whom she could communicate this sudden revelation. But Amy had gone, leaving a note that she would be back at four, and the young waiter who brought her breakfast tray only grinned nervously when she tried to tell him how simple life was.

"When you're tired, you sleep."

"Si, señora."

"When you're hungry, you eat. Simple, logical, basic."

"Si, señora, but I'm not hungry."

"Oh, what the hell," Wilma said. "Go away."

The waiter had almost ruined her revelation, but not quite. She opened the balcony doors and addressed the warm, sunny afternoon: "I shall be absolutely basic all day. No fuss, no frills, no getting upset. I must concentrate only on the essentials."

The first essential was, obviously, food. She was hungry, she would eat.

She removed the cover from the ham and eggs. They were black with pepper, and the tomato juice tasted strongly of limes. Why in God's name did they have to put lime juice on everything? It was difficult enough to be basic, without fools and incompetents thwarting you at every corner.

I am hungry, I will eat turned into *I am hungry, I must eat* and finally *I'll eat if it kills me.* By that time she was no longer hungry. The revelation joined its many predecessors in oblivion and life once more became, as it always had been for Wilma, complex and bewildering.

Later in the afternoon Amy returned with an armload of packages. She found Wilma in the sitting room reading a copy of the *Mexico City News* and drinking a Scotch and soda.

Wilma peered over the top of her spectacles. "Buy anything interesting?"

"Just a few little things for Gill's children. The stores were jammed. It seems funny, everyone shopping on Sunday." She put her packages on the coffee table beside the silver box. "How are you feeling?"

"All right. I must have passed out like a light after the doctor gave me that junk."

"Yes."

"What did you do all evening?"

"Nothing."

Wilma looked faintly exasperated. "You can't have done nothing. Nobody does nothing."

"I do. I did."

"What about dinner?"

"I didn't have any."

"Why not?"

"I was—upset." Amy sat down stiffly on the edge of a green leather chair. "The box came."

"So I see."

"It looks very expensive."

"It was," Wilma said. "The least they could have done was wrap it. My purchases are my own private business."

"Not this one."

"Obviously not." Wilma tossed the newspaper on the floor and took off her spectacles. She couldn't read without the spectacles, since she was far-sighted, but she could see across the room better without them. Amy's face looked pale and numb. "I gather you noticed the initials?"

"Yes."

"And concluded, of course, that Rupert and I are madly in love; that we have, in fact, been carrying on an affair for years and years behind your..."

"Shut up," Amy said. "I hear the girl in the bedroom."

Consuela had let herself in with her passkey and was now making up the beds. Her shoulders slumped and her feet dragged from weariness because she'd had a fight with her boyfriend that had lasted well into the night. The cause of the fight was, to Consuela, absolutely ridiculous. All she did was pilfer a black nylon slip from 411, but her boyfriend became very angry and told her she would lose her job and accused her of trying to steal the smell off a goat if she got the chance. Besides all that, the slip had been too small for her and she'd torn the seams attempting to force it over her hips.

Life was unfair. Life was cruel as a bull's horn. Consuela groaned as she changed the sheets, and made small suffering sounds as she slopped a little water around the washbasin. *Why would I steal the smell off a goat?*

"You're jealous," Wilma said softly. "Is that it?"

"Of course not. It just doesn't seem proper to me. And if Gill finds out he'll make a big fuss about it."

"Don't tell him, then."

"I never tell him things. But he always finds out in some way."

"Why do you still care what your brother thinks, at your age and weight?"

"He can cause a lot of trouble," Amy said. "He's always been suspicious of Rupert anyway. I don't know why."

"I could tell you why, but you wouldn't like it. You probably wouldn't even listen."

"Then why bother telling me?"

"I'm not going to." Wilma finished her drink. "So you don't care whether I give Rupert the box, just so long as Gill doesn't find out about it. That's very funny."

"Not to me, it isn't. And I don't see why you had to buy such an expensive gift in the first place."

"Because I wanted to. You wouldn't understand. You haven't done anything because you *wanted* to in your whole life. I have. I do. I saw this box in the window of a little shop and it reminded me of something Rupert said once, that the sea looked like hammered silver. I never really understood what he meant until I saw the box. So I bought it. I simply went in and bought it, without thinking of money, or you, or Gill, or all your weird, complicated…"

"Not so loud. The girl…"

"The hell with the girl. The hell with the box, too. Take the damn thing and throw it over the balcony!"

"We can't very well do that," Amy said quietly. "There are too many people on the street. Someone might get hurt."

"But that's what you'd like to do, isn't it?"

"I don't know."

"Oh, admit it. Admit something for a change. You want to get rid of the box."

"Yes, but…"

"Do it then. Chuck the thing over the railing. That'll be the end of it. And good, good riddance."

In the bedroom Consuela let out a little bleat of protest. To throw a silver box out into the street like garbage would be a terrible sin. Suppose someone very rich saw it falling through the air and caught it and became even richer—Consuela groaned at the thought of such injustice and cursed herself for her stupidity in pretending to the two ladies that she couldn't speak English. Now she could not present herself to them and state her case: I am a very poor and very humble peasant. Sometimes I am even tempted to steal...

No, that would not have been good, giving them ideas about her stealing. Perhaps it was just as well that she had pretended not to know English. This way she could simply confront the ladies, looking very poor and humble and honest, and they might offer to give her the box.

Consuela glanced in the mirror above the bureau. How did one go about looking honest? It was not easy.

She picked up the carpet sweeper and headed for the sitting room, already making plans for the silver box. She would sell it and buy lottery tickets for tomorrow's drawing. Then, on Tuesday morning when her winning number was published in the papers, she would tell her boyfriend to go kiss a goat, thumb her nose at the hotel manager, and leave immediately for Hollywood where she would have her hair bleached and walk among the movie stars.

She spoke in Spanish, sounding very poor and humble. "If the good ladies will excuse me, I have come to clean the room."

"Tell her to go away and come back later," Wilma said.

Amy shook her head. "I don't know how."

"I thought you took Spanish in high school."

"That was over fifteen years ago and only for a semester."

"Well, find the book of common phrases for tourists."

"We—I left it on the plane."

"Oh, for God's sake. Well, get rid of her some way."

Consuela had discovered the silver box on the coffee table and was making excited noises over its beauty, its craftsmanship, and the number of lottery tickets it was worth.

"She must be talking about the box," Amy said.

"Let her talk."

"If you're just going to throw it away anyway, you could give it to her instead."

"I could," Wilma said, "but I won't. And who said I intended throwing it away?"

"You did. You practically promised."

"Nothing of the sort. I said if *you* wanted to throw it away you were to go ahead and do it. But you didn't have enough nerve, so you lost your chance. The box is mine. I bought it for Rupert and I'm giving it to Rupert."

Consuela, cheated out of her blond hair and her movie stars, squawked in protest and held her hand against her heart as if it were breaking.

Wilma glared at her. "Go away. We're busy. Come back later."

"Oh, you are a wicked one," Consuela moaned in Spanish. "A selfish one, a bad one. Oh, may you spend eternity in hell."

"I can't understand a word you're saying."

"Oh, I wish you could, you black witch with the evil eye. Children grow pale and sicken when you look at them. Dogs put their tails between their legs and slink away…"

"I've had enough of this," Wilma said, addressing Amy. "I'm going to the bar."

"Alone?"

"You're perfectly welcome to come along."

"It's so early, barely five o'clock."

"Then stay here. If you can dig up some of that high school Spanish of yours, I'm sure you and the girl can have a ball."

"Wilma, don't drink too much when you're in this mood. It will only depress you."

"I'm already depressed," Wilma said. "*You* depress me."

At seven o'clock Amy set out to look for her.

The hotel operated two bars, an elaborate one on the roof with a lively orchestra, and a smaller one between the lobby and the dining room for people who preferred martinis without music. Amy tipped the elevator boy two pesos and asked him what direction Wilma had taken.

"Your friend in the fur coat?"

"Yes."

"First she went up to the roof garden. A little time later she came down again. She said the marimbas made it too noisy to talk."

"Talk?" Amy said. "To whom?"

"The American."

"What American?"

"He hangs around the bar. He is what you call homesick, for New York. He likes to talk to other Americans. He is harmless," the boy added with a shrug. "A nobody."

They were at a table in a corner of the crowded bar, Wilma and the harmless American, a dark-skinned, blond-haired young man in a garish green and brown striped sport coat. Wilma was doing the talking and the young man was listening and smiling, a trained professional smile without warmth or interest. He looked harmless enough, Amy thought. And he probably was—except to Wilma. Two marriages and two divorces had taught Wilma nothing about men; she was both too suspicious and too gullible, too aggressive and too vulnerable.

Amy crossed the room uncertainly, wanting to turn back, but wanting even more to be reassured that Wilma was all right, not drunk, not nervous. *This is the wrong place for her. Tomorrow we'll go to Cuernavaca as the doctor suggested. It will be more restful, there will be no homesick Americans.*

"Why, there you are," Wilma said, very loudly and gaily. "Come on, sit down. I'd like you to meet a fellow San Franciscan. Joe O'Donnell, Amy Kellogg."

Amy acknowledged the introduction with a slight nod and sat down. "So you're from San Francisco, Mr. O'Donnell?"

"That's right. But call me Joe. Everybody does."

"I somehow got the impression you were from New York."

O'Donnell laughed and said easily, "Woman's intuition?"

"Partly."

"Partly the sport jacket, maybe. I had it tailored in New York. Brooks Brothers."

Brooks Brothers, my foot, Amy thought. "Indeed? How interesting."

"Let's have a drink," Wilma said. "You sound too sober, Amy dear. Sober and mad. You're always getting mad; you just don't show it like the rest of us."

"Oh, stop it, Wilma. I'm not mad."

"Yes, you are." Wilma turned to O'Donnell and put her hand on his sleeve. "You want to know what she's mad about? Do you?"

"I can take it or leave it," O'Donnell said lightly.

"Sure you want to know."

"You're drunk."

"A little. A very very very little. Make up your mind. Do you want me to tell you what she's mad about?"

"All right, spill it and get it over with."

"She thinks—Amy is always thinking, it's a very bad habit—she thinks I have designs on her husband because I bought him a silver box."

O'Donnell grinned. "And have you?"

29

"Of course not," Wilma said vigorously. "Rupert's like a brother to me. Besides, I *like* to buy things for people. Sometimes, when I'm feeling good, that is. Other times I get depressed and stingy and I wouldn't give the time of day to a blind man."

"Right now you're feeling good, eh?"

"Very good. Let me buy you a drink. Or perhaps you'd like a silver box?"

"We could start with the drink."

"O.K. Waiter! Waiter! Three tequilas with lime."

"Wilma," Amy said. "Listen. Why don't we go and have dinner?"

"Later, later. I'm not hungry right now."

"I am."

"*You* go and have dinner, then."

"No. I'll wait for you."

"All right, wait. Just don't sit there looking mad. Try to be cheerful."

"I'm trying," Amy said grimly, "harder than you think."

O'Donnell's smile was becoming a little strained. The evening wasn't turning out as he'd planned—a few free drinks, some talk, perhaps a small loan. One woman he could usually handle nicely. Two women, especially two women who didn't like each other, might become a burden. He wished there were some quick, quiet way of ditching them both without any hurt feelings. Hurt feelings could result in complaints to the manager, and he didn't want the welcome mat pulled out from under him. The bar was his headquarters. He never got into any trouble. The Americans who came in were always glad to set up drinks for a fellow Friscan or New Yorker or Chicagoan or Angeleno or Milwaukeean or Denverite. Some of the cities he claimed as home he had visited. The others he'd read about or heard about. He'd never been to San Francisco but he'd seen many pictures of the Golden Gate

Bridge, Fisherman's Wharf and the cable cars. That was enough real information. The rest he could fake, including an address if he was asked for one. He always used the same address, Garden Street, because every city had a Garden Street.

"Eleven-twenty-five Garden Street," he told Amy. "You probably never heard of it. It's over on the east side of town. Or it was. They may have torn the whole district down by now and put up hotels or department stores. Are the cable cars still running?"

"Some of them," Amy said.

"It makes me homesick just thinking about them."

"Does it?" She wondered what place he was really homesick for; a farm in Minnesota, perhaps, or a little desert town in Arizona. She knew she would never find out. She couldn't ask and he wouldn't tell. "Is there anything to stop you from going home, Mr. O'Donnell?"

"Just a small matter of money. I've had some bad luck at the track."

"Oh."

His smile widened until it seemed almost genuine. "Yes. I'm a naughty boy, Mrs. Kellogg. I gamble. I have to."

"Oh?"

"There's no other way of making money. I can't apply for any job without working papers and so far I haven't been able to get any working papers. Say, this is beginning to sound like Be-Sorry-For-Joe O'Donnell night. Let's can it. Let's talk about you. What have you two ladies been doing for amusement in Mexico City?"

"Amusement?" Wilma lifted her brows. "I hardly know the meaning of the word any more."

"We'll have to change that. How long will you be here?"

"We leave tomorrow," Amy said. "For Cuernavaca."

"That's too bad. I was hoping to show you…"

31

"Cuerna—who?" Wilma said loudly to Amy.

"Cuernavaca."

"And we leave tomorrow?"

"Yes."

"Are you out of your mind? We just got here. Why in God's name should we take off for a place I never even heard of, Cuern—whatever it is?"

"Cuernavaca," said Amy patiently.

"Stop repeating it. It sounds like a disease of the spine."

"It's supposed to be very beautiful and…"

"I don't care if it's the original Garden of Eden," Wilma said. "I'm not going. What put such a crazy idea in your head anyway?"

"The doctor suggested it, for the sake of your health."

"My health is fine, thank you. You look after your own."

The drinks came and O'Donnell sat without embarrassment while Wilma paid for them. A year ago, or two years, he might have been a little embarrassed. Now he was merely tired. The two ladies were, as he'd feared, becoming a burden. He wished they would go to Cuernavaca right away, tonight.

He said firmly, "No visitor to Mexico should miss Cuernavaca. Cortés' palace is there, and the cathedral, just about the oldest cathedral in the republic. And birds, thousands of singing birds. If you like birds."

"I hate birds," Wilma said.

He went on to describe the climate, the tropical foliage, the beautiful plazas, until he realized that neither of the two women was paying the slightest attention to him. They had begun to argue again, about a man called Gill, and what Gill would think if he walked in right now, or if he ever found out.

O'Donnell got up and left.

*

32

Consuela quit work at eight o'clock and went down to the service entrance where her boyfriend was supposed to meet her. He wasn't there, and one of the kitchen help told her he'd gone to the jai alai games.

Consuela cursed his pig eyes and his black heart and returned to her broom closet, determined on revenge. It wasn't much of a revenge but it was all she could think of, to stay in the closet all night and let him worry about her and wonder why she didn't come home and where she was.

She made herself as comfortable as possible on a bed of towels. There was no ventilation in the closet but Consuela didn't mind this. The night air was bad anyway. It caused consumption, and if you had consumption you couldn't get into the United States. The immigration authorities wouldn't give you any papers.

She dozed off and dreamed that she was on a bus going to Hollywood. Suddenly the bus stopped and a bearded man who looked a little like Jesus opened the door and said, "Consuela Juanita Magdalena Dolores Gonzales, you have consumption. You must get off the bus immediately." Consuela flung herself at his feet, weeping and pleading. He turned away from her sternly, and she began to scream.

When she first woke up she could hear herself screaming, but a moment later, sitting up, fully awake now, she realized it was not herself she'd heard screaming. It was one of the ladies in 404.

In spite of the lateness of the hour there were a dozen eyewitnesses who'd been passing on the *avenida* below the balcony of 404, each of them eager to give his version of what had happened.

The American lady paused at the railing and looked down before she jumped.

She did not look down. She knelt and prayed.

She didn't hesitate a moment, just ran across the balcony and dived over.

She screamed as she fell.

She didn't make a sound.

She carried in her arms a silver box.

Her arms were empty, flung wide to the heavens in supplication.

She turned over and over in the air.

She fell straight down and head first, like an arrow.

The eyewitnesses all agreed on one point: when she struck the pavement she died instantly.

In the hotel manager's office Dr. Lopez gave a brief statement to the police. "I treated Mrs. Wyatt last night for a case of *turista*. An unhappy woman. Very nervous, very high-strung."

"Very drunk," said the bartender.

"Very rich," Consuela said with a nervous giggle. "What a pity to die when one is rich."

The doctor held up his hand for silence. "Kindly allow me to finish. My rounds begin in less than five hours and even a doctor requires some sleep. As I said before, you'll get the complete story from Mrs. Kellogg when she recovers. How soon that will be depends on the hospital authorities. She's suffered a bad shock. Moreover, when she fainted she struck her head on the bedpost, so she may have some degree of concussion as well. That's all I can tell you."

"I, too, am very nervous and high-strung," said Mercado, the older of the two policemen. "Still, I do not leap off balconies."

Dr. Lopez smiled without amusement. "You might one day, one balcony. Good morning, gentlemen."

"Good morning, Doctor. Now you, Consuela Gonzales. You

claim you were in the broom closet and heard a woman scream-ing. Which woman?"

"The small, brown-haired one."

"Señora Kellogg?"

"Yes."

"Was she just making a noise or was she screaming words?"

"Words. Like 'stop' and 'help.' Maybe others."

"Just as a matter of curiosity, what were you doing in the broom closet at that hour?"

"Sleeping. I was very tired after work. I work hard, very very hard." She threw a glance at Escamillo, the manager of the hotel. "Señor Escamillo doesn't realize how hard I work."

"That I don't," Escamillo said with a snort.

"No matter, no matter, no matter," Mercado said. "Go on, señorita. You woke up and heard screaming. You rushed into 404. And?"

"The small one, Señora Kellogg, was lying on the carpet beside the bed. Her head was bleeding and she was unconscious. I couldn't see the other one anywhere. I never thought to look over the balcony. How could I think of such a thing? To take one's own life, it is a mortal sin." Consuela crossed herself, fearfully. "The room smelled of drinking and there was half a bottle of whiskey on the bureau. I tried to give the señora some to wake her up but it just spilled all over."

"So you drank the rest yourself," said Escamillo, the manager.

"The merest drop. To keep my strength up."

"Drop. Ha! You reek of it," said Señor Escamillo.

"I will not be insulted by any pig of a man!"

"So you dare to call me a pig of a man, you *ladronzuela*!"

"Prove it. Prove I am a *ladronzuela*!"

Mercado yawned and reminded them that it was late; that he and his colleague, Santana, were very tired; that he, Mercado,

35

had a wife and eight children and many troubles; and would everybody, please, be friendly and cooperative? "Now, Señorita Gonzales, when you failed to rouse the señora, what did you do?"

"I telephoned down to the room clerk and he sent for the doctor. Dr. Lopez. He has an agreement with the hotel."

"He has a contract," Escamillo said. "Signed."

Consuela shrugged. "Does it matter what you call it? When a doctor is necessary, it is always Dr. Lopez they send for. So he came. Immediately. Or very soon anyway. That is all I know."

"You stayed with the señora until the doctor arrived?"

"Yes. She did not wake up."

"Now, señorita, what do you know of a silver box?"

Consuela looked blank. "Silver box?"

"This one. See, it has blood on it and is badly dented where it struck the pavement. Have you ever seen this box before?"

"Never. I know nothing about it."

"Very well. Thank you, señorita."

Consuela rose gracefully and crossed the room, pausing for a moment in front of Escamillo's desk. "I do not take insults. I quit."

"You don't quit. You're fired."

"I quit before I was fired. So ha!"

"I shall count every single towel," Escamillo said. "Personally."

"Cochino."

Consuela snapped her fingers and went out, slamming the door firmly and finally behind her.

"You see?" Escamillo cried, beating the air with his fists. "How can I run a hotel with help like that? They are all the same. And now this terrible scandal. I am ruined, ruined, ruined. Policemen in my office! Reporters in my lobby! And the Embassy—Mother of Jesus, must the Embassy be brought into this, too?"

"We must, of course, inform the Embassy in such cases," Mercado said.

"These crazy Americans, if they want to jump do they not have places to jump in their own country? Why must they come here and ruin an innocent man!"

Everyone agreed that it was most unfair, most sad, but God's will, after all. No one could argue with God's will, which was responsible for national and domestic disasters like earthquakes, unseasonable rains, temperamental plumbing, difficulties with the telephone exchange, as well as cases of sudden death.

It was comforting having someone to blame, and Escamillo was beginning to feel better when another point suddenly occurred to him. "What of the suite, 404? It is empty and yet it is not empty. I must charge for it or lose money. But I cannot charge if there is no one in it. And I cannot put anyone in it while the señoras' belongings are still there. What must I do?"

"You must learn not to think so much of money," Mercado said firmly and picked up the silver box and nodded to his colleague, Santana. "Come along. We will examine 404 once more and then lock it until the little señora recovers."

The balcony doors had been left open but the suite still reeked of whiskey, from the carpet where it had spilled and from the bottle itself which Consuela had left uncorked on the bureau.

"It would be a shame," Mercado said, reaching for the bottle, "to let this product stand here and evaporate."

"But it is evidence."

"Evidence of what?"

"That the señora was drunk."

"We already know from the bartender that she was drunk. We must not accumulate too much evidence. It would only confuse matters. The case is, after all, quite simple. The señora

37

was drinking much *tequila* and became depressed. *Tequila* is not for amateurs."

"Why did she become depressed?"

"Unrequited love," Mercado said without hesitation. "Americans make much of these things. It is in all their cinemas. Have a nip."

"Thank you, friend."

"One thing we can be sure of. It was not an accident. I thought at first, the señora, after drinking heavily, may have rushed out to the balcony to get some air, perhaps also to relieve her stomach. But this is not possible."

"How is this not possible?"

"She would never, in such an emergency, stop to pick up the silver box." Mercado sighed. "No. She killed herself, poor lady. It is a sad thing to think of her wandering around in hell, is it not?"

Dawn was breaking through a gray drizzle.

"It rains," Santana said.

"Good. It will wash off the sidewalk and drive the people home."

"There are no more people. It is all over."

"Amen," Mercado said. "Still I wonder, along with Señor Escamillo, why did she jump from this particular spot with all the American places to choose from."

"The Empire State Building."

"Of course. And the Grand Canyon."

"The Brooklyn Bridge."

"Niagara Falls."

"And others."

"Many others." Mercado closed the balcony doors and locked them. "Well, one must not argue with the will of God."

"Amen."

4

Rupert Kellogg's office was on the second floor of a new concrete building that stood just on the edge of Montgomery Street's ancient prestige. Here he ran a small accounting business with the aid of his secretary, Pat Burton, a spinster addicted to changing the color of her hair, and an apprentice, a young man named Borowitz who was working his way through San Francisco State College.

Rupert was forty, a tall, bland-faced, soft-talking man who'd been in the accounting business for nearly twenty years. He was moderately efficient, and moderately successful, in his work, but he didn't enjoy it. He would have preferred to do something more interesting and amusing, to own a pet shop, for instance. He had a profound love for animals and an intuitive understanding of them. The hours he spent at Fleishhacker Zoo seemed to him to be full of the fundamental meanings of life, but he never told this to anyone, not even his wife Amy; and the only time he'd suggested the possibility of opening a pet shop there'd been such a rumpus among his in-laws that he'd given up the idea. At least he'd given up mentioning it. It was still in the back of his mind, hidden away like a deformed child from the disapproving gaze of his brother-in-law.

On Monday morning he arrived late at the office, a habit that was growing on him, especially since Amy had left. Miss Burton, pumpkin-haired for the beginning of the autumn season, was on the telephone looking distraught. This she did easily and with so little provocation that Rupert paid no attention. He found Miss Burton's anxiety states more tolerable if he stayed beyond their boundaries as much as possible.

"Hold on, operator. He's just this minute coming in the door." Miss Burton pressed the telephone dramatically to her chest. "Thank God you've come! A Mr. Johnson in Mexico City wants to talk to you."

"I don't know any Mr. Johnson in Mexico City."

"He's from the American Embassy. It must be terribly important. You don't suppose something awful has…"

"Isn't this the wrong time to suppose, Miss Burton? I'll take the call in my office." He closed the door behind him and picked up the phone. "Rupert Kellogg speaking."

"One moment, please, Mr. Kellogg. All right, go ahead. Here's your party, Mr. Johnson."

"Mr. Kellogg? This is the American Embassy in Mexico City, Johnson speaking. I have bad news to report so I might as well give it to you now and straight."

"My wife…"

"Your wife's going to be all right. It's her companion, Mrs. Wyatt. She's dead. To be quite blunt about it, she went on a drinking spree and killed herself."

Rupert was silent.

"Mr. Kellogg, are you still there? Operator, I've been cut off. Operator! *Telefonista!* For the love of the Lord, couldn't I make just one phone call without interruption? *Telefonista!*"

"You haven't been cut off," Rupert said. "I was—this is a—shock. I—I have known Mrs. Wyatt for many years. How did it happen?"

Johnson told him what details he knew, in a sharp, disapproving voice, as if he considered Wilma's death a breach of international etiquette.

"And my wife?"

"She's suffering from shock, naturally. They've taken her to the American British Cowdray hospital. Do you want that address?"

"Yes."

"It's Mariano Escobedo, 628. The telephone number is 11-49-00."

"Will she be able to talk to me if I call?"

"Oh no. She's under sedation. She has a head injury incurred when she fainted, nothing serious as far as I know."

"How long will she be in the hospital?"

"It's impossible to tell," Johnson said. "Do you have any friends here who could look after her?"

"No. I'd better come down myself."

"That's a good idea. Shall I call the Windsor Hotel where she was staying and ask them to hold the suite for you?"

"Please," Rupert said. "I'd also appreciate it if you left a message at the hospital for her: I'll be down there tonight."

"What if you can't make it tonight?"

"I'll make it. There's a flight leaving in two hours. My wife took it last week."

"Do you have a tourist card? They won't let you on the plane without one."

"I'll get one."

"Very well. I'll leave the message for her. One more thing, Mr. Kellogg. The police were unable to find any next of kin to Mrs. Wyatt. Has she any relatives?"

"A sister in San Diego."

"Name?"

"Ruth Sullivan."

"Address?"

"I don't know where she's living, but her husband is a lieutenant commander attached to the Eleventh Naval District. It shouldn't be hard to find out his home address. Earl Sullivan."

"Thanks, Mr. Kellogg. And if there's anything the Embassy can do for you while you're down here, let me know. The number is 39-95-00."

"Thank you. Good-bye."

"Good-bye."

Miss Burton appeared in the doorway, slump-shouldered and spaniel-eyed, as befitted the gravity of the situation. "I couldn't help overhearing, people talk so loud over long distance."

"Do they?"

"That's a terrible thing about Mrs. Wyatt, dying in a foreign country like that. All I can say is, God rest her soul." It seemed enough. Miss Burton straightened her shoulders, put on her spectacles and said briskly, "I'll call Western Air Lines right away."

"Yes."

"Are you feeling all right, Mr. Kellogg?"

"I—certainly. Certainly."

"I've got some aspirin."

"Take them yourself."

Miss Burton knew better than to argue. She merely dropped two aspirins on his desk and went out to the reception room to phone the air lines. Rupert stared at the aspirins for a long time. Then he got up and went over to the water cooler and swallowed them both at once.

Miss Burton sailed in on a note of elation. "Success. You leave on flight 611. But goodness, the arguing I had to do. Some snip of a clerk kept saying that the people leaving on 611 were already checking in at the airport. And I said, listen, this is an emergency. I spelled it right out for him, e-m-e-r-g-e-n-c-y... Oh, I see you took the pills. Good. How are you fixed for money?"

"I'll need some."

"O.K., Borowitz can run over to the bank. Now, here's your schedule. Depart International at 11:50. Lunch on plane. Stopover

42

in L.A. for about an hour. Leave L.A. at 2:30. Dinner on plane. Arrive Mexico City at 10:10, Central Standard Time."

Miss Burton might go to pieces over smaller crises, but when the larger ones came along she expanded to meet them. She arranged for money, tourist card, toothbrush, clean socks and pajamas, care of the Scottie, Mack, and message to Amy's brother, Gill Brandon. When she finally got Rupert on the plane and he waved good-bye to her from the window, she was moist-eyed but relieved, like a mother sending her son off to school for the first time.

She drove Rupert's car back to the city and parked it in the garage of his house on 41st Avenue. Then she let Mack out to run while she washed and dried the dishes Rupert had left in the sink. In all the years she'd worked for him, this was only the second time she'd been inside his house, and it gave her a curious feeling, like watching somebody sleeping.

After she finished the dishes she wandered through each of the rooms, not snooping really but merely taking mental notes like any good secretary interested in her boss: *Mahogany and lace in the dining room, that's too formal for him, must be her doing… I'll bet he sits in the yellow chair, there are hair oil marks on the back and a good lamp beside it. He loves to read, he'd need a good lamp… A grand piano and an organ, fancy that. She must be musical, he can't whistle a note… I'll never get used to those colored johns… The maid's room, I bet. Every bit as nicely furnished as the others, which goes to show how generous he is. Or maybe it's her. Borowitz says she comes from a very moneyed family… The hall table looks like genuine rosewood, the kind you polish with your bare hands if you're crazy that way and have lots of time. A post card. I wonder who from. Well, post cards aren't private. If you've got something private to say, say it in a letter.*

Miss Burton picked up the post card. It bore a colored photograph of the Old Faithful geyser on one side and a penciled message on the other.

Dear Mr. and Mrs. Kellogg:

I am having a real good time on my holiday. I saw Old Faithful already six times. It is a site. It gets cold here at nite, blankets needed. There is a swimming pool that smells bad owing to minrals in the water. The smell don't come off on you fortunately. No more room on the card. Hello to Mack.

Yours truly,

GERDA LUNDQUIST.

Yellowstone yet, Miss Burton thought. And I can't even afford Sequoia. Not that I want to. People are always saying how small you feel under the big trees, which isn't my idea of fun at five foot one-half inch.

Having finished her unofficial tour of the house and mail, Miss Burton let the Scottie in at the back door and fed him several dog biscuits. Then she walked over to Fulton Street to catch a bus back to town.

She had no premonition of disaster. The day was sunny and her horoscope that morning had been exceptionally favorable. So had Rupert's, which she always looked up even before her own: THIS IS A WONDERFUL DAY FOR YOU LEOS AND LIBRANS.

Wonderful day, Miss Burton thought, and skipped along the sidewalk, quite forgetting that Mrs. Kellogg was in a hospital and Mrs. Wyatt was dead.

The plane was on schedule. Rupert called the A.B.C. Hospital from the airport and made arrangements to see his wife in spite of the lateness of the hour.

44

He arrived at the hospital shortly before midnight and was met at the main desk by a dark young man who identified himself as Dr. Escobar.

"She's asleep," Escobar said. "But I think, under the circumstances, it would do her good to see you. She has called for you several times."

"How is she?"

"That's difficult to say. She's been crying a great deal, whenever she wakes up, in fact."

"Is she in pain?"

"Her head may hurt a bit, but I think the crying is explained more by emotional reasons than physical ones. It is not merely the death of her friend that has disturbed her, though that certainly is bad enough in itself. There were additional circumstances, the fact that the two women were alone in a strange city without friends, that they'd been drinking a good deal…"

"Drinking? Amy has never taken more than a cocktail before dinner."

Escobar looked a little embarrassed. "There is considerable evidence that both your wife and Mrs. Wyatt had been drinking *tequila* with an American barfly named O'Donnell. The women had a loud argument."

"They were very good friends," Rupert said stiffly. "Ever since childhood."

"Very good friends sometimes argue together, sometimes drink together. What I am trying to tell you is that Mrs. Kellogg feels extremely guilty, guilty about the drinking, guilty about the argument, guilty, most of all, because she was unable to prevent her friend's suicide."

"Did she try?"

"Anyone would try, naturally."

"Has she told you what…"

"She's told me very little. She has very little to tell. *Tequila* is a formidable concoction if one is not used to it." Escobar turned to the elevators. "Come along, we'll see her now. We've moved her from Emergency to a private room on the third floor."

She was asleep with the night light on. Her left eye was black and swollen, and there was a bandage over her temple. Crumpled pieces of Kleenex littered the floor beside her bed.

"Amy." Rupert bent over his sleeping wife and touched her shoulder. "Amy, dear, it's me."

She was hardly awake before she began to cry, holding her fists against her eyes.

"Amy, don't. Stop that, please. Everything's going to be all right."

"No—no…"

"Yes, it is. I'm here to take care of you."

"Wilma's dead." Her voice began to rise. "Wilma's dead!"

Escobar stepped swiftly over to the side of the bed and grasped her hand. "Now, Mrs. Kellogg, no more hysterics. The other patients on the floor are sleeping."

"Wilma's dead."

"I know," Rupert said. "But you must think of yourself now."

"Take me home, take me out of this terrible place."

"I will, dearest. Just as soon as they let me."

"Come now, Mrs. Kellogg," Escobar said smoothly. "This isn't such a terrible place. We'd like to keep you here for a few days of observation."

"No, I won't stay!"

"For a day or two…"

"No! Let me go! Rupert, get me out of here. Take me home!"

"I will," Rupert said.

"All the way home? To my own home and Mack and everything?"

"All the way, I promise."

It was a promise which, at the moment, he intended to keep.

5

Gill Brandon came downstairs wearing his composite morning expression: anticipation over what the day would bring and suspicion that something was bound to spoil it.

He was a short, stocky, vigorous man with a forceful manner of speaking that made even his most innocuous remark seem compelling, and his most far-fetched theory sound like a self-evident truth. To heighten this effect he also used his hands when he talked, not in any dramatically loose European style, but severely, geometrically, to indicate an exact angle of thought, a precise degree of emotion. He liked to think of himself as mathematical and meticulous. He was neither.

Gill kissed his wife, who was already at the table with the morning paper in front of her opened to the lovelorn column. "Any phone calls?"

"No."

"It's damned peculiar."

"What is?" Helene said, knowing perfectly well what was, since Gill had talked of nothing else for a week. Thank God it was Monday and he had to go into the city to work. If the stock market was fluttery, so much the better. It would take his mind off other things. "Here's a terribly funny letter from some woman in Atherton. I wonder if it's anyone we know. It could be Betty Spears. Listen. 'Dear Abby: My problem is my husband is so stingy that he even snitches my green stamps.' I know for a fact Johnny Spears saves green stamps…"

"Will you *listen* to me?"

"Of course, dear. I didn't know you were saying anything."

"Rupert's been down there for a week now and I haven't heard a word since that first phone call from his secretary. Not a word about how Amy is and what's going on, when they'll be back, nothing."

"He may be busy."

Gill scowled at her across the table. "Busy doing what, may I ask?"

"How should I know?"

"Then stop making up nonsensical excuses for him. Nobody's too busy to pick up a phone. He's damned inconsiderate. And what Amy ever saw in him I'll never know."

"He's very good-looking. And very nice."

"Good-looking. Nice. Great Scott, is that what women marry men for?"

"You're hungry, dear. I'll ring for breakfast."

Helene pressed the buzzer under the table, feeling a mild surge of power. She had been born and raised in an Oakland slum, and never, in all her twenty years of marriage, had she become accustomed to the miracle of ringing for anything she wanted. Breakfast, martinis, chocolate creams, tea, magazines, cigarettes—you pressed a button, and bingo, whatever you wanted, there it was. Sometimes Helene just sat and thought of things to want so she would have the pleasure of pulling the tasseled bell cord or pressing the buzzer underneath the table.

Occasionally she visited Oakland but more frequently her parents came down the Peninsula to see her, Mrs. Maloney wearing her teeth and Sunday clothes, Mr. Maloney sober as a judge and dry as a herring. After the initial greetings of genuine pleasure, both parents stiffened into silence, too stunned by the luxurious surroundings to do much of anything except sit and stare. Back home they were affectionately voluble about their daughter Helene, who had gone to Mills College on a scholarship and lived in a fine house in Atherton with her wealthy husband and three beautiful children.

Face to face with her, they became mute and embarrassed, and their visits were a nightmare, especially to Gill, who tried harder than Helene did to make the Maloneys feel at home. His tactics were peculiar: he sought to minimize his wealth by calling attention to some of his economies, by talking forcefully of having his thirteen-year-old son take a paper route and his seventeen-year-old daughter work her way through college. The result of this stratagem was more confusion on the part of the Maloneys and complete frustration for Gill, who meant, as usual, only to do the right thing. No one had ever been able to figure out why such good intentions as Gill's often had such disturbing consequences.

"Amy's association with the Wyatt woman," Gill said, "has meant nothing but trouble. She was obviously unbalanced. Anyone but Amy would have seen that and avoided her."

Helene mentally crossed herself. "Now Gill. *De mortuis*... Besides, they were friends. You don't go back on a friend because she's having, well, a few emotional problems. Wilma could be a very charming and entertaining person when she wanted to. That's the way I prefer to remember her."

"You have a very simple and convenient memory."

"And I intend to keep it that way. Eat your breakfast."

"I'm not hungry," Gill said irritably. "Personally, I'm inclined to blame Rupert for this whole business. He should have vetoed the trip as soon as the subject was broached. Two women wandering alone around a foreign, uncivilized country—why, it's preposterous."

It sounded rather pleasant to Helene whose traveling was confined to shopping trips to the city and summers at Tahoe. She munched on a piece of crisp bacon, listening to Gill the way one listens to waves breaking on a beach, knowing the noise will always be the same, only varying in volume now and then with the tides and the weather.

So often the noise was about Amy, and Helene listened out of habit, without interest. In her opinion, Amy was a dull little creature, invested with wit by her brother and beauty by her husband, and having, in fact, neither. Helene, too, had often wondered about the relationship between Amy and Wilma, but she wondered from quite a different point of view from Gill's: why should such an intense and energetic person as Wilma have wasted so much time on a mouse like Amy?

Gill turned up his volume. "I still think the American Embassy should have called me about this unfortunate affair."

"Why?"

"Amy's my kid sister."

"She is also a grown woman with a husband. If she needs looking after, let Rupert do it."

"Rupert is incapable of handling certain situations."

"What's to handle?" Helene said blandly.

"There are probably decisions to be made, actions to be taken. Rupert's too soft. Now if I were down there I'd be firm with those foreigners."

"If you were down there, dear, you'd *be* the foreigner."

"I suppose you think that's terribly clever?"

"It's just the truth."

"You seem," he said with a dry little smile, "to be hitting on a great many truths these days."

"Oh, I am. Some large, some small."

"Tell me a few of them."

"Another time. You'd better hurry if you're going to take El Camino instead of Bayshore." She smiled at her husband across the table. In spite of his manner of talking she knew him for a gentle man, more like Amy than he would ever realize. "You'll drive carefully, won't you, Gilly?"

"I wish you wouldn't call me that. It sounds absurd."

"You don't object when Amy calls you…"

"It was my nickname when we were children. She uses it unconsciously. And I do object. Remind me to speak to her about it when she comes home."

Helene's expression didn't change, but she felt a sudden sick feeling in her stomach and the coffee she was drinking seemed to have turned sour. *I don't want her to come home. She is two thousand miles away. I like it this way.*

David, the thirteen-year-old, bounced into the room, wearing the uniform of the military day school he attended. "Morning, all."

"What on earth," Helene asked, "is the matter with your face?"

"Poison oak," he said cheerfully. "Roger and Bill got it, too, when we were out on maneuvers. Boy, the sergeant was mad. He said the Russians could have landed while the whole bloody bunch of us were chasing around after poison oak."

"I'll call for you after school and take you to the doctor."

"I don't want to go to any bloody doctor."

"Stop saying that word. It's not very nice."

"The sergeant uses it all the time. He's an Englishman. They always say bloody. Oh, I forgot to tell you, Uncle Rupert's home. He phoned last night when you were out."

"You might," his father said, "have told me before."

"How could I, when you were out?"

"Is Amy all right?"

"I don't know. He didn't say anything about her."

"Well, what *did* he say?"

"Just that he was going to be home all day today and would like to see you about something important."

"I'll call right…"

"He said not to call. It's a very private matter. He wants to talk to you in person."

Gill was already on his feet.

The two men shook hands and Gill said immediately, "Amy's all right?"

"Yes."

"Where is she? Still in bed?"

"She's—we can't talk out here. You'd better come in."

The house was dark and quiet and musty, as if the people who lived there had been away for a long time. No sun filtered through the drawn blinds, no sound crept past the closed windows. Only in the den, at the end of the long, narrow hall, had the drapes been pulled open, and the morning sun hung dusty in the air. On the tiled coffee table was a half-empty highball glass smudged with lipstick, and beside it, an unstamped envelope with the name "Gilly" written across the front in Amy's boarding-school script.

Gill stared at it. The letter was wrong; the silent man at the window, the too-quiet house, the half-empty glass, all seemed ominous. He cleared his throat. "The letter—it's from Amy, of course."

"Yes."

"Why? Why a letter, I mean."

"She preferred to do it that way," Rupert said, without turning.

"Do what?"

"Explain why she went away."

"Went away? Where?"

"I don't know where. She refused to tell me."

"But this is preposterous, it's impossible."

Rupert turned to face him. "All right, have it your way. It's preposterous and impossible. It happened, though. Some things *can* happen without your knowledge or permission."

They glared at each other across the sunny room. When Amy was around to smooth things over, the two men had been civil to each other and observed the amenities. Now, without her presence, the unspoken gibes and unvoiced criticisms that had accumulated through the years seemed to hang between them, ready to be plucked out of the air and used as strings to either bow.

"She took her clothes," Rupert said, "and her dog, and left."

"The dog, too?"

"It was hers. She had a right to."

"Taking the dog, that means…"

"I know what it means."

They both knew. If Amy had intended to come back, she wouldn't have taken the dog with her.

"You'd better read your letter," Rupert said.

Gill picked it up and held it in his hands for a moment, very carefully, as if it were a bomb that might detonate at any sudden movement. "Do you know—what's in it?"

"It's sealed and addressed to you. How should I know?" He did know, though. He remembered every word in the letter. He'd gone over it a dozen times looking for flaws. He'd found some, but only after it was too late.

Gill read slowly, mouthing the words like a beginning reader.

Dear Gilly:

    I have told Rupert to give you this letter, rather than mailing it, because I know you will want to ask him questions.

Some he'll be able to answer, some he won't. Some even *I* can't answer, so how can I make you understand the reasons why I am going away for a while? The main thing is, I am. It is a very big decision for me. I can't phone you to say good-bye because I know you'd argue with me and I'm afraid my decision might not be strong enough to stand up under an argument from you.

It is a week now since Wilma died, a week of regret and grief, but also one of reexamination of myself. I didn't come out very well. I am thirty-three, and it seems that I've been living like a child, always leaning on other people. I didn't enjoy it, I just could never get around to not leaning. I never will, if I simply stay here and sink back into the same old rut. I must get the feeling of being alone and being myself. I know that if I had been a mature, responsible person, used to making decisions and acting on them, I would have been able to prevent Wilma's death. If I had not been drinking myself, I could have stopped Wilma from drinking to the point of depression...

"She'd been drinking," Gill said in surprise. "How much?"

"A lot."

"That doesn't sound like the Amy I know."

"Perhaps there's another one. She was not only drinking, she was drinking in the company of an American barfly named O'Donnell."

"I don't believe it."

"That's your privilege."

...All this may seem nonsensical to you, Gilly. But I can be practical, too. I have given Rupert the necessary authority to handle my financial affairs, so you needn't worry on that score. And please, Gilly, whatever you do, don't blame Rupert for my going away. He's been a wonderful husband to me. Be *kind* to him, cheer him up, he's going to miss me. You will, too, I know, but you have Helene and the children. (Give them my love and tell them I've gone east to recuperate or some such thing. Don't tell them I've gone off my rocker which is probably what you're thinking. I haven't gone off, I'm just getting on.)

Best love, and don't worry about me!

AMY.

Gill returned the letter to its envelope, slowly and methodically, as if it were a bill he was thinking twice about paying. "Has she been doing much talking along these lines the past week?"

"Quite a bit."

"Then she had planned on leaving even before she came home?"

"She came home to pick up Mack."

"You should have warned me ahead of time, sent me a wire or something. I might have prevented this."

"How?"

"By telling her not to go."

"That's the pattern she's trying to break out of," Rupert said, "being told what to do."

"Have you any idea where she went?"

"No. I'm not even sure she had a definite place in mind."

"Well, how did she leave?"

"She called a cab, but I persuaded her to cancel it and let me drive her to the station."

"What time?"

"About eight."

"Is there any possibility she was coming down to Atherton to see me?"

"None," Rupert said. "She wrote you the letter, for one thing. For another, she had Mack with her. There are no baggage cars on the commuters' trains to accommodate animals."

"There are on the Lark. It leaves for Los Angeles around nine o'clock. By God, that's it, that's where she is, Los Angeles."

"There are trains *leaving* as well as arriving at Los Angeles."

"Even so, she shouldn't be too difficult to trace, a young woman traveling by train with a bad-tempered Scottie."

"Mack's not bad-temp—Oh, for heaven's sake, get it through your head, Gill. Amy doesn't *want* to be traced."

"She's a woman. Half the time women don't know what they want. They have to be told, guided. I've always thought you should have kept a firmer hand on the reins."

"Funny, I thought you were holding them."

Gill colored. "What do you mean by a remark like that?"

"Just what I said. The reins were never in my hands. Nor have I ever considered my wife in the same category as a horse."

"Horses and women have a lot in common. Put them in an open field and they run to hell and gone."

"Where did you learn so much about women, Gill?"

"I don't want to quarrel with you," Gill said firmly. "The situation is too serious. What are you going to do about it?"

"Nothing. What do you suggest I do?"

"Call the police. Tell them to locate her and bring her back."

"On what grounds? Amy's of age, considerably overage, in fact."

"We'll be able to think of some reason."

"Oh, for... All right. Suppose we do and suppose they find her. What then?"

"They'll bring her home and we'll have an opportunity to talk some sense into her head."

"By 'we' I presume you mean 'you'?"

"Well, I've always been able to handle her, make her see reason."

"Perhaps she *is* seeing reason," Rupert said. "Her own. Not yours."

Gill struck the arm of the davenport with his fist. Particles of dust scurried up and away in alarm. "You're being pretty damn cool and collected for a man whose wife has disappeared."

" 'Disappeared' isn't quite the word."

"It is to me."

A sudden draft rippled the moted shafts of sunlight, and a woman's voice called out from the back door, "Mack. Here, Mack. Come on, boy. Time for your run."

At the first word Gill had risen expectantly, but as the woman continued to call the dog he sat down again heavily as if he'd been pushed in the chest by Rupert's fist. Rupert had not moved.

"Here, Mack. Come on, now. If you're on that bed again I'm going to tell on you! Mack? Boy?"

Miss Burton appeared in the doorway, her cheeks pink with cold, her hair bleached to the color and texture of straw. "Why, Mr. Kellogg. My goodness. Why, I had no idea you were home. Barging in like this, what must you think of me?"

"It's all right, Miss Burton," Rupert said. "I should have given you advance notice. You know Mr. Brandon, of course?"

"Why, yes. Good morning, Mr. Brandon."

Gill rose and nodded briefly. He'd seen Miss Burton at least a dozen times but he would never have recognized her meeting her casually on the street. She seemed to assume different faces and personalities with each new hair color. Only her voice remained the same, brisk brunette, no matter how blond her inanities.

58

Miss Burton fondled Rupert with her eyes. "This is such a nice surprise finding you home. I just came by to give Mack his breakfast and take him for a run, and lo and behold, here you are instead. My goodness. How is Mrs. Kellogg?"

"She's fine, thank you," Rupert said.

"Where's Mack? Now that I'm here I might as well…"

"You run along to the office, Miss Burton. I'll—take care of Mack."

"All rightie, whatever you say."

"I'll be down this afternoon sometime."

"Good. Things are getting a mite behind. Borowitz has a new girlfriend and can't concentrate. She's absolutely nothing to look at, just young."

"Yes. Well. You'd better run along now, Miss Burton."

"I'll do that. Good-bye, Mr. Brandon. It was real nice seeing you again. And you'll be along later then, Mr. Kellogg?"

"Yes."

"My, I'm glad you're back. Borowitz is making a real fool of himself."

After she'd gone Gill said heavily, "What are you going to do about Amy?"

"Wait."

"Just sit on your rear and wait?"

"That's right."

"You're a fool."

"That's your opinion."

"You're damned right it is," Gill said and stamped furiously out of the room and down the hall to the front door.

I handled him wrong, Rupert thought. *He may do something crazy, like go to the police.*

6

On Friday of the same week, when Rupert returned from lunch, he found Helene Brandon waiting for him in his office. She was wearing a sable-trimmed suit and matching hat, and she carried the commuters' essential, an enormous handbag. She had obviously been passing the time going through the handbag. Half its contents were on Rupert's desk: paperback books, a magazine, two pairs of spectacles, cigarettes, pills, a candy bar, a collapsible umbrella, plastic rain boots and a pair of low-heeled black shoes.

The feminine clutter reminded Rupert of Amy and he tried to avoid looking at it by keeping his eyes fixed on Helene's face. A pretty face, round and plump and without secrets.

She began thrusting everything back into her handbag. "Gill would have a cat fit if he knew I was here, so it goes without saying that I'm not, eh?"

Rupert smiled. "For a lady who isn't even here you're looking very pretty."

"We Peninsulans have to dress to the teeth when we come to the city just to prove we haven't gone to seed in the suburbs."

"That hardly seems likely in Atherton."

"Oh, you think not? Listen, I haven't had on a pair of high heels for weeks. My feet are killing me."

"Change your shoes."

"No, I'd rather suffer. I'll enjoy the trip more in retrospect if I suffer now."

"That's logic, I presume?"

"No. It's just true." She snapped the handbag shut and said with no change of tone, "I know about Amy. Gill told me."

"I'm glad he did. I wanted you to know."

"You haven't heard from her?"

"I didn't expect to. She told me she wouldn't be writing for a time."

"She could at least let you know where she is."

"She could, yes," Rupert said. "But she hasn't. And I'm not in a position where I can tell her what to do."

"Maybe that's what she wanted."

"What is?"

"To be where people can't tell her what to do. I wouldn't mind it myself for a few weeks." Helene contemplated this idea with half-closed eyes. Then she dropped it, with a sigh, and said abruptly, "Listen. Gill's spoiling for trouble. I thought I'd better warn you."

"What kind of trouble?"

"I'm not sure… You'd better close the door. If Miss Burton's ears perk up any further she'll take off in the first high wind."

"I have no secrets from Miss Burton."

"Well, *I* have," Helene said dryly. "And you might be going to."

Rupert closed the door. "What does that mean?"

"Gill has ideas."

"About what?"

"You and Miss Burton."

Rupert let out an explosive sound like an angry laugh. "Oh, for Christ's sake!"

"I think it's funny too, but I'm not laughing. Gill's dead serious. He's managed to convince himself that you don't want Amy back because you have—other interests."

"What possible basis could he have for such a screwy idea?"

"Miss Burton has a key to your house."

"Naturally. I gave it to her so she could feed Mack twice a day while I was away."

"Gill said you usually put him in a kennel."

"The last time we left him in a kennel he picked up mange."

"You see? There's a logical explanation for everything but Gill just won't believe it. He's practically irrational on the subject of family. I don't know why, and I prefer not to think about it since there's nothing I can do about it."

"I often think about it," Rupert said.

"So do I, really. It's useless, though. We might just as well say 'Gill is a nice guy but he's nuts on the subject of Amy,' and let it go at that."

"Consider it gone."

Helene took a deep breath to signify that that subject was closed and another about to be opened. "Then there's the lipstick."

"What lipstick?"

"On the highball glass in the den. Gill says it was exactly the same shade as Miss Burton was wearing."

"And thirty million other American women. It was a new color introduced last spring, something or other sherbet."

"Tangerine sherbet?"

"Right. I gave it to Amy for Easter in one of those fancy doodad cases. Now is that all?"

"Not quite."

Rupert struck his palms together in helpless fury. "What else, for God's sake?"

"I wish you wouldn't keep swearing. It upsets me. And if *I* get upset heaven knows what will happen. I seem to be the only calm one in the whole caboodle. Now what was I going to say?"

"I'd be a fool to guess," Rupert said grimly and sat down behind his desk to wait while Helene sorted through her mind, as she had sorted through her handbag, coming across all sorts of odds and ends she thought she'd lost.

"I should have taken notes, but I couldn't very well because Gill thought he was talking to me in confidence. I mean, he had no idea I'd come here and tell you. He'd have a cat fit if it..."

"You said that."

"Did I? Well, it only goes to show. Oh, I remember now. The cigarette butts in the den."

"There were no cigarette butts in the den."

"That's just it. None in the ash trays, none in the fireplace. Amy's a very heavy smoker—it's one of the few things she's ever defied Gill about. And since she was particularly nervous that night, Gill said you'd expect to find all the ash trays overflowing."

"With fifty years of training, Gill might make a detective."

"Well, he *does* notice things," Helene said defensively, "even if they turn out to be wrong."

"Even if, yes. In this case he didn't notice far enough. Amy spent no more than five minutes in the den. He should have taken the trouble to examine the rest of the house. Tell him that next time he's to bring his microscope."

"You're mad, aren't you?"

"You're damn right I'm mad. What's he trying to prove?"

"Nothing definite. He just thinks you're not telling the truth."

"The truth about what?"

"Everything. I warned you, he's simply not rational."

"That's a quaint way of putting it. The man's a maniac."

"Only where Amy is concerned."

"Isn't that enough?" Rupert pounded the desk with his fist in a half-conscious imitation of Gill. "Ever since Amy and I have been married he's been trying to break us up. He's been sitting around hoping I'd beat her or chase other women or turn into a lush or a drug addict, anything. Anything at all, just so Amy would leave me and climb back into the family nest like a goddamn baby bird. Well, he's half succeeded. She's left me, but she didn't head back for the nest."

"She hasn't left you, Rupert. Not really. I—I read the letter." She flushed slightly and twisted one of the rings on her plump fingers. "Gill asked me to read it."

"Why?"

"He wanted my opinion about whether it made sense—female sense, as he called it—and about whether I thought the handwriting was, well, authentic."

"And was it?"

"Of course. I told Gill the handwriting was unmistakably Amy's. Only…"

She paused, working at the ring again as if it had shrunk in size and was hurting her. It was the diamond Gill had given her twenty years ago. Amy had still been in the nest then, baby bird Amy, featherless, formless, her mouth constantly open not because of hunger, bird-style, but because of a bad case of adenoids. The adenoids had been removed, feathers grew, wings developed; but there'd been no place to fly until Rupert came along. Helene remembered Amy's wedding day more clearly, and more happily, than her own. *Bye bye, blackbird.*

"Only what?" Rupert said.

"He didn't trust my judgment. Yesterday he took the letter to a handwriting expert, a private detective named Dodd."

Rupert leaned forward, mute with shock. From Borowitz's office next door came the spasmodic coughing of the adding machine. Business as usual, Rupert thought, Borowitz feeding figures into the machine and coming up with answers. And a few blocks away, in another office, Gill was coming up with answers too, only there was something the matter with his machine, a loose screw. "What," he said finally, "does he think has happened to Amy?"

64

"He's not thinking, he's *feeling*, don't you see that? None of his ideas makes sense. That's why I came here, to warn you. Also because I'm worried, I'm worried sick. It's not good for Gill's health to have these ideas."

"It's not good for mine either, obviously. Tell me some of these ideas of his."

"You won't get mad again?"

"I can't afford to. The situation's too serious."

"All right then. He said last night he's not sure Amy ever came home at all."

"Then where is she?"

"Still in Mexico."

"Doing what?"

"Doing nothing. He thinks—no, I don't mean thinks, I mean feels. He *feels* she's dead."

Rupert didn't even look surprised. The surprises were over, he knew now Gill was capable of anything. "A psychiatrist would have a ball with that one. Has he managed to feel how she died?"

"No."

"Or when?"

"During the week that you were down there."

"So I went to Mexico City," Rupert said, sounding very detached, "and killed my wife. Did I have any particular reason?"

"Money. And Miss Burton."

"I wanted to inherit Amy's money and marry Miss Burton, is that it?"

"Yes." She had managed to work the ring off her finger. She sat now with it in her lap, not looking at it, only partly conscious that it was there. "Oh, he doesn't really believe all this, Rupert. He's hurt because Amy didn't confide in him, and angry at you for letting her go away."

"There's more to it than that. You oversimplify. Why do you suppose Gill feels that Amy is dead?"

It was a question she'd been avoiding in her own mind for several days, and it disturbed her to hear it spoken aloud. "I don't know."

"Because he wants her dead."

"That's not true. He loves her. He loves her best."

"He also hates her best. She is—or he believes she is—the source of his emotional troubles. If Amy's dead, his problems are over. He's free. Oh, sure, he'll suffer at the conscious level, he'll feel grief and pity and all that, but down at rock bottom he's free." He paused. "Only he isn't. She's not dead."

"I never thought for a minute that she was." But Helene looked relieved to hear it, guiltily relieved. It was as if she, too, scraping along rock bottom, grubbing for satisfactions, had come across a dead Amy, a drowned, bedraggled baby bird with its mouth still open. "Listen, Rupert. You seem to understand that Gill isn't—himself. You'll be tolerant, won't you?"

"That depends."

"On what?"

"How far he goes."

"I'm sure the worst is over. When something upsetting like this comes along Gill thrashes around for a while but he eventually sees reason." She had convinced herself, if not Rupert. She picked up the ring from her lap and put it back on her finger, only partly aware that she'd taken it off in the first place. "I must go now. I'm late for a dental appointment. You'll let us know right away if you hear from Amy?"

"Certainly. I'll even bring the letter over so Gill can have the handwriting analyzed."

"Don't be bitter."

66

"I'm not. I'm quite serious about it. What have I got to lose?"

"You're being an awfully good sport over all this," Helene said warmly. "I think Amy's made a terrible mistake, walking out on you."

"She didn't walk. I drove her. And if she made a mistake, that's her business. For her to do anything on her own is a good thing, even if it's wrong. Perhaps eventually Gill will understand that."

"He will, give him time."

"She's never done anything on her own before. The trip to Mexico City was intended to be a declaration of independence. But it was merely a change in dependence: Wilma planned every inch of the way."

Helene mentally crossed herself at the mention of Wilma, whom she hadn't really liked very well but who at least had never appeared in her dreams as a dead bird. "Listen, Rupert. You may think this is silly, but have you thought about advertising for Amy in some of the big newspapers throughout the country? I mean, let her know we're worried and want to know where she is. You see ads like that all the time: Bill, contact Mary; Charley, write to Mother; Amy, come home. Things like that."

"Amy, come home," he repeated. "Gill's idea, I suppose?"

"Well, yes. But I agree with it. It might do some good. Amy isn't the type who'd want people to worry about her unnecessarily."

"Perhaps she is. How do we know? She's never had much of a chance to prove what type she is."

"You could try advertising anyway. It can't do any harm. There wouldn't even be any publicity if you made the ad vague enough and didn't mention last names. We certainly don't want publicity."

"You mean Gill doesn't."

"I mean *none* of us does," she said sharply. "This whole business—it would look very queer in the newspapers."

"It won't take long to reach the papers if Gill goes around sounding off that Amy is dead and I'm about to establish a love nest with Miss Burton."

"So far he's sounded off only to me."

"And to the private detective, Dodd."

"I don't think he told Dodd much, just enough to make it plausible that he wanted the handwriting in Amy's letter compared to other samples of her writing." She got up and leaned across the desk. "I'm on your side, Rupert, you know that."

"Thanks."

"But you have to make some concessions to Gill for your own protection. If he thought you were really *trying* to find Amy and get her back, it would help put him straight. So try."

"Advertise, you mean?"

"Yes."

"All right, that's easy enough."

"The library should have the names of all the leading newspapers in the country." She hesitated. "It might be quite expensive. Naturally, Gill and I will pay for..."

"Naturally?"

"Well, it was our idea. It's only fair that..."

"I think," Rupert said, "that I can afford to advertise for my own wife."

Amy, come home. He could already see the letters in print, but he knew Amy never would.

7

Elmer Dodd was a brash, bushy-haired little man, who'd been, at various times and with varying success, a carpenter in New Jersey, seaman on a Panamanian freighter, military policeman in Korea, bodyguard to a Chinese exporter in Singapore, and Bible salesman in Los Angeles. When, at forty, he met a woman who persuaded him to settle down, he found himself experienced in many things and expert in none, so he decided to become a private detective. He moved his bride to San Francisco. Here he hung around the Hall of Justice to get the feel of things, attended trials, where he took notes, and haunted the morgues of the *Chronicle* and the *Examiner*, where he read up on famous criminal cases of the past.

All this might eventually have helped, but it was sheer coincidence that set him up in business. He was having a snack one day in a spaghetti joint in North Beach when the proprietor shot his wife and mother-in-law and the mother-in-law's boyfriend. Dodd was the sole surviving witness.

During the years that followed, Dodd's name became familiar to every newspaper reader in the Bay area. It popped up in divorce cases, felony trials, gossip columns and, more regularly, in the personal section of the want ads where he offered his services as an expert in various fields, including handwriting analysis. He owned a couple of books on the subject, which, in his own opinion, made him as much of an expert as anyone else since handwriting analysis was not an exact science. He knew enough, at any rate, for run-of-the-mill cases like this Amy business.

Amy sounded like a bit of a nut (Dodd also owned a book on abnormal psychology), but nut or not, she had certainly written all four of the letters Gill Brandon had brought in for comparison. Dodd had known this immediately, even before Brandon had left his office. But it would have been impractical to admit it. Experts took time, they checked and rechecked, and were suitably reimbursed for their trouble. Dodd took a week, during which he checked and rechecked Gill Brandon's financial standing and decided on a fee. It was just enough to make Brandon squawk in protest, but not so much as to cause him to refuse payment.

Dodd was satisfied.

So, in spite of the fee, was Gill. "I don't mind telling you, Dodd, that this is a great load off my mind. Naturally, I was almost positive she wrote the letter. There was only a small element of doubt."

What a liar, Dodd thought. "Which is now dispelled, of course?"

"Of course. As a matter of fact, we heard from her again yesterday. By 'we' I mean she wrote to her husband and he forwarded her letter to me."

"Why?"

"Why? Well, I—he realizes I'm very concerned about my sister. He wanted me to know she is all right."

"And is she?"

"Certainly. She's in New York. I should have guessed she might go there—we have relatives in Queens and Westchester."

"Did you bring the letter with you?"

"Yes."

"I'd like to see it. There'll be no extra charge, of course," Dodd added, after a quick study of Gill's expression. "I'm just curious."

Gill passed the letter across the desk, reluctantly, as if he were afraid that Dodd might suddenly alter his opinion and claim all the letters were forgeries.

Dodd knew at first sight that the handwriting was identical with that in the other letters, but he went through a few motions for Gill's benefit. Using a magnifying glass and a ruler, he measured and compared spaces between lines and words, margins, paragraph indentations. It was, however, the text of the letter that interested him: it seemed so much sharper and more positive than any of the others. The handwriting was the same, certainly. But was the woman?

Dear Rupert:

Whatever made you do such an absurd thing? I couldn't believe my eyes when I saw the ad in the *Herald Tribune*. Gill will be furious if he finds out. You know how livid he gets at the mere mention of publicity.

Of course I'll come home. But not right away. As you can see by the postmark, I'm in New York. It's a good place to be when you want to figure things out by yourself. Everyone lets you alone. For the time being, this is just what I need.

Don't worry about me. I miss you, but in a way I'm quite happy and I know this is what you would want for me.

Please take that advertisement out of the paper. (Or is it papers? I hope to heaven not!) Also, please phone Gill and Helene and tell them everything's fine. I'll write to them eventually. This business of writing is very difficult for me—it seems to bring before me so clearly and sharply some of the very things I'm trying to forget—not forget, but get away from. The old Amy was a baby and a bore, but the new one isn't quite sure of herself yet!

Mack is fine. There are quite a few dogs in New York, mostly poodles, but we meet the odd Scottie now and then, so Mack is not lonesome.

Before I forget, the Christmas card list is in the top left drawer of the desk in the den. Order the cards early and have both our names printed on them, naturally.

Take care of yourself, dear. Love,

AMY.

"Christmas card list," Dodd said without expression. "This is September."

"I taught Amy—that is, we were both brought up to attend to such matters well in advance."

"Isn't this overdoing it a bit?"

Gill knew it was, but he asked, "What do you mean?"

"It sounds to me as if she doesn't intend to be home for Christmas and is trying to tell you in a nice way."

"I can't believe that."

"Well, you don't have to," Dodd said cheerfully. "Maybe it's not true. Have you talked it over with your brother-in-law?"

"No."

"I suggest you do. He's probably better acquainted with his wife than you are."

"I doubt that. Besides, Rupert and I are not exactly on the best of terms."

"Family friction, eh? Maybe that's the real reason Amy decided to leave town."

"There was no family friction until she left. Some has developed since, of course."

"Why 'of course'?" When Gill didn't answer, Dodd went on, "Cases like this are a lot commoner than you might imagine, Mr. Brandon. Most of them don't get as far as the police files or the newspapers; they're kept within the family. A lady gets bored or disgusted or both, and off she goes on a bit of a winging. When

72

the wingding is over, she comes home. The neighbors think she's been on a holiday, so nobody's any the wiser. Except maybe her. Wingdings can be rough on a lady."

Dodd was an expert on wingdings, without owning any books on the subject.

"My sister," Gill said, "is not the kind of woman who would be interested in wingdings." He coughed over the unfamiliar word as if it had stuck in his throat like a fishbone. When he had finished coughing he wiped his mouth and stared at Dodd, suddenly hating the bushy-haired little man with his metallic eyes and his tarnished, keyhole views of the back bedrooms of life.

He rose without speaking, not trusting his voice, and reached for the letters on Dodd's desk.

"No offense intended," Dodd said, observing Gill's trembling hands and the bulging veins in his temples with detachment. "And none given, I trust?"

"Good day."

"Good day, Mr. Brandon."

That night at dinner Dodd's wife asked, "How was business today?"

"Fine."

"Blond and beautiful?"

"That's strictly in books, sweetheart."

"Glad to hear it."

"Mr. Brandon is neither blond nor beautiful," Dodd said, "but he's interesting."

"How so?"

"He has a problem. He thinks his sister was murdered by her husband."

"And what do you think?"

"Nobody's paid me to think," Dodd said. "Yet."

8

On Sunday, the twenty-eighth of September, three days after Gill's visit to Dodd, the Kelloggs' maid, Gerda Lundquist returned from her month's vacation in Yellowstone National Park.

She called Rupert from the bus depot in the hope that, since it was Sunday and he wouldn't be working, he might offer to come and pick her up. No one answered the telephone so she grudgingly took a taxi. The vacation had been hard on her pocketbook, and on her nerves too, especially toward the end when the snows began and people swarmed out of the park, leaving it to the bears and the chipmunks and the antelopes for the winter. Gerda was looking forward to a nice pay check and some warm, cozy evenings in front of the television set the Kelloggs had given her the previous Christmas. Television was so restful she often went to sleep watching it, and Mrs. Kellogg would come to her door and rap softly and ask, "Gerda? Did you forget to turn off the television, Gerda?" Mrs. Kellogg never commanded, never gave a direct order. She asked politely, "Would you mind…" or "What do you think of…", as if she respected Gerda's superior age and wider experience in life.

She let herself into the house with her latchkey and went immediately out to the kitchen where she filled the teakettle with water to heat for some Postum and a boiled egg. The kitchen was very clean, the dishes washed, the sink shining, signs that Mrs. Kellogg must be home from Mexico. Mr. Kellogg was more willing than able around the kitchen.

As the kettle began to hum, so did Gerda, an old song from her childhood in Minnesota, the words of which had long since been forgotten. She did not hear Rupert come in, she was only aware of a sudden change in the room, and she turned and saw him standing in the doorway to the hall. His hair was disheveled, and his face and ears were pink with wind as if he'd been running in the park with Mack.

He stared at her in silence for a few seconds. He seemed to be trying to figure out who she was and what she was doing in his house. Then he said, "Good evening, Gerda," in a flat voice with no welcome in it.

"Good evening, Mr. Kellogg."

"How was the vacation?"

"Oh, it was grand. But I don't mind telling you it's good to be back home."

"I'm glad to have you back."

But he didn't sound glad or look glad, and Gerda wondered what she had done to displease him. *How could I have done anything? I was in Yellowstone. Ach, it's just one of his moods. Not many people know about his moods.* "How's Mrs. Kellogg?" she said carefully. "And Mack?"

"Mrs. Kellogg is away on another holiday. She took Mack with her."

"But..." The kettle began to whistle as if in warning. Gerda compressed her lips and busied herself at the stove, trying not to look at the wooden peg beside the back door where Mack's red and black plaid leash was hanging. She could feel Mr. Kellogg's eyes pointing at her back like a double-barreled gun.

"But what, Gerda? Go on."

"I wasn't about to say anything. Would you care for an egg, Mr. Kellogg?"

"No thanks. I've had supper."

"Eating in restaurants for so long like I did makes you hungry for something real homey like a soft-boiled egg."

The egg cracked in the boiling water. Gerda added a pinch of salt to the water so the egg white wouldn't all drool out of the shell. Her hand was shaking and some of the salt spilled on the stove, turning the blue flame of gas momentarily to orange. *That's Mack's leash hanging by the door. He's a well-behaved dog, the best, but no one would ever take him out without his leash because of the traffic. Especially not Mrs. Kellogg. She's nervous about cars. She's never even learned to drive.* She said aloud, "Have you been eating in restaurants or at home while Mrs. Kellogg is away?"

"Half and half."

"I must say you've kept the kitchen real nice and neat."

"Miss Burton dropped by this morning on her way home from church and helped clean up."

"Oh," Gerda said. Miss Burton, that creature with the dyed hair. On her way home from church, was she, and what were the churches coming to these days, pray tell?

She took the egg out of the saucepan and put it in an egg cup. Then she buttered a piece of bread and sat down at the table to eat. Mr. Kellogg was still standing in the doorway watching her with that funny expression in his eyes. It made her so nervous she could hardly swallow.

"By the way," Rupert said, "you'll be interested to know that Mack left in high style. My wife brought him a new leash from Mexico, one of those fancy, hand-tooled leather jobs."

"Well, isn't that nice."

"Mack thought so."

"I bet he looked too cute for words."

"Yes." Rupert stepped back with a grimace as if he'd had a sudden twinge of pain. "When you've finished eating, I'd like to have a talk with you, Gerda. I'll be in the den."

The talk turned out to be quite simple. She was fired. No reflection cast on her abilities, of course. A matter of simple economics. Mrs. Kellogg would be away in the East indefinitely, and it just wasn't feasible to keep Gerda on. He made a lot of nice remarks about her efficiency and cooperation and so on, but it all amounted to one thing: she was fired. A month's wages in lieu of notice and the best of references, which Miss Burton would type up and have waiting for her at the office. Good-bye and good luck.

Gerda said, "You mean you want me to leave right away?"

"Yes."

"Right now *tonight?*"

"It might be simpler that way," Rupert said, "since you haven't unpacked yet. I'll drive you wherever you want to go."

"I got no place to go."

"There are hotels. And the Y.W.C.A."

Gerda thought of the warm, cozy evenings in front of her television set, now suddenly to be replaced by cold, deadly ones in the lobby of the Y.W.C.A. with a lot of other women as dull as herself. Resentment stabbed her eyes until they bled tears.

"Now, Gerda," Rupert said uneasily. "You mustn't cry. This isn't actually a personal matter."

"It's personal to me!"

"I'm sorry. I wish—well, we all wish things could be different."

"This is a terrible home-coming."

"There have been worse," Rupert said, remembering his own.

"What about the TV set?"

"That belongs to you. I'll have a man come to disconnect it and deliver it to you when you get settled."

"If I get settled."

"I'm sure you'll have no difficulty finding another job, one you'll enjoy more. Things would be pretty dull for you around here without Mrs. Kellogg and Mack. I suggest you try an employment agency."

Gerda sniffed. She didn't like employment agencies and the snippy way they asked questions and pretended that jobs were scarce just to make themselves look good when they got you one. "I think I'll call the Brandons."

"Who?"

"The Brandons, Mrs. Kellogg's brother and his wife. They got that big place to keep up in Atherton and many's the time I've heard her complain how she couldn't get decent help."

He didn't say anything. He just kept staring at her as if he thought she'd lost her mind.

Flushing, Gerda said, "Maybe you think I wouldn't fit into such a fancy place, me and my country ways, is that what you're thinking? Well, let me tell you I heard Mrs. Brandon with my own ears call me a jewel. That was no more than three months ago, and if I was a jewel three months ago I guess I'm a jewel right here and now."

"Of course. Of course you are," Rupert said, and he kept his voice very quiet because he felt like screaming. "I happen to know, however, that Mrs. Brandon has a complete staff at the moment."

"That's not saying she will have tomorrow or next week, things being like they are in this world."

"You might not like living on the Peninsula."

"The climate's nice. All this fog in the city is hard on my bronchial tubes. That's my weakest spot."

"The Brandons have three children. They're very noisy."

"A little noise won't hurt me none." She turned to leave. "Well, I better go find some cartons so I can pack the rest of my stuff."

"Gerda. Wait."

She looked back, surprised at the urgency in his voice. "Yes sir?"

"I'll call Mrs. Brandon, if you like, and ask her if she has an opening and what salary she's prepared to pay and so on."

"I don't want to put you to any trouble."

"It's no trouble at all."

"Well, that's real kind of you, Mr. Kellogg. I'm much obliged, I'm sure,"

"I might as well call now, while you're still here, and get the matter settled." He gave her a dry little smile. "You may even enjoy working at the Brandons'. Everyone to his taste."

While she was in her room packing the rest of her things she could hear him talking on the main phone in the kitchen. His voice was very loud and distinct, and she wondered if Helene Brandon was possibly getting a little deaf.

"Helene? This is Rupert… Fine. And you?… Glad to hear it… Oh, she's having a great time, seeing every play in New York. Helene, the reason I called is Gerda. She returned from her vacation tonight, and I had to tell her that I couldn't afford to keep her on. She's first-rate at her job, as you know… A jewel. Yes, she remembered that you called her that when you were talking to Amy some time ago… I can't help it if Amy will be mad. It's a matter of simple economics… I can eat most of my meals in restaurants and hire a cleaning woman once a week. To get back to the subject of Gerda…"

Gerda, the jewel, fought a brief brisk battle with Gerda, the woman. The woman emerged victorious and tiptoed down the hall to the extension telephone in the master bedroom. She had no need to lift the receiver to hear Rupert; his voice veritably boomed from the kitchen. Mrs. Brandon must certainly be getting deaf. Or perhaps she always had been and covered it up by lip reading.

Gerda's hand, slowed by guilt, reached for the telephone. *I really shouldn't. I'm a jewel…*

"I thought it would be nice if we kept Gerda in the family, as it were… I realize you don't need anyone right now, Helene… Frankly, I think you'd be missing an excellent opportunity if you didn't snap her up. Her qualifications are most unusual, you know that for yourself. I think she'd be good with the children, too… Of course, if you haven't a place for her, you haven't…"

Meticulous as a surgeon, Gerda lifted the receiver. The dial tone buzzed in her ear. For a second she thought that Mrs. Brandon had, in sudden pique or boredom, hung up. Then she heard Rupert's voice again from the kitchen: "Naturally she'll be disappointed. So am I. But we can't ask you to do the impossible, Helene… Yes, I'll tell her to try you again in a few months. Goodbye, Helene."

9

"This Gerda Lundquist," Dodd said, rubbing his chin, "she's reliable?"

Until the past twenty-four hours Gill Brandon had barely been aware of Gerda's existence; he was not competent to answer the question. But because he wanted to believe her, he nodded vigorously. "Absolutely reliable. I'd trust her with my life."

Dodd smiled the dry little smile that indicated disbelief in practically everybody. "There are a lot of people I'd trust with my life that I wouldn't trust to give an accurate account of something they saw or experienced."

"Miss Lundquist is not an imaginative type. Nor would she have any reason for trying to put my brother-in-law in a bad light."

"Revenge for being fired?"

"She already has a better job," Gill said stiffly.

"With you?"

"With us."

"Why?"

"Why? We needed an extra servant, that's why."

That's not why, Dodd thought. *Now that he's got the first shred of evidence against his brother-in-law he intends to keep it in a safe place. I'm glad I'm not in Kellogg's shoes. This Brandon means business.*

Gill said, "You understand, Gerda knows nothing about Amy's disappearance. She thinks that Amy is simply on a vacation in New York."

"And you think she isn't?"

"I know she isn't. I told you previously we have relatives in Queens and Westchester. I called both places last night after

Gerda had come to us with her story. No one has seen or heard from Amy."

"That proves nothing."

"It would if you knew Amy. She's always been very conscientious about keeping in touch with members of the family. If she were anywhere near New York she would have called Cousin Harris or Aunt Kate. Whether she wanted to or not, she would have contacted them out of duty."

"How long is it since you've seen your sister?"

"She left for Mexico City on the third of September, a Wednesday. I said good-bye to her the previous day."

"Was she acting normally?"

"Of course."

"In good spirits?"

"Excellent. Very excited at the prospect of the trip, like a kid who's never been any place on her own before."

"Was Mrs. Wyatt with her at the time?"

"Yes. They'd been doing some last-minute shopping and called me from the St. Francis to come and have lunch with them."

"What kind of woman was Mrs. Wyatt?" Dodd asked.

"Eccentric. Oh, some people found her very amusing, and I think Amy was rather fascinated by her, in the sense that she never knew what Wilma would do next." He added grimly, "She does now."

"Yes, I guess she does. What day was it that Mrs. Wyatt killed herself?"

"A little over three weeks ago, on a Sunday night, the seventh of September. I was informed the following day when Miss Burton, Rupert's secretary, called me at my office. Rupert went down to Mexico City that same day, the seventh."

Dodd wrote the dates in a notebook, more because he wanted something to do than because he thought he'd ever be referring to them again. Still a firm believer in wingdings, he was convinced that Amy would pop up one of these days with an unlikely everything-suddenly-went-black story.

"I heard nothing from him," Gill continued, "until a week later. I was out that night, but he left a message with my son that I was to come to the house to discuss something important. When I got there he told me Amy had left and gave me her farewell letter, the one I first brought to you. You may recall its contents."

"Yes."

"She wrote that she'd been drinking the night of Wilma's death."

"And?"

"Rupert added something to that. He told me she'd been in the company of an American barroom hanger-on named O'Donnell. I think he was lying. My sister is cultured, well bred. No well-bred woman would walk into a bar and pick up…"

"Wait a minute, Mr. Brandon," Dodd said. "Let's get something clear. If I'm to find your sister it's more important to me to know her faults than her virtues. She may be kind and gentle and sweet and so on. That doesn't tell me a thing. But if I know she has a weakness for barflies named O'Donnell, then I start looking up all the barflies named O'Donnell in my files."

"Your humor isn't very funny."

"It wasn't intended to be. I was making a point."

"You may consider it made," Gill said coldly. "It doesn't alter the facts, however. My sister has no weaknesses of the kind you mean. Besides, Rupert has been proved a liar."

"You're referring to Gerda Lundquist's account of his pretended telephone conversation with your wife?"

"Among other things, yes."

"Why do you think he falsified that call?"

"It's obvious. He wanted to prevent Gerda from making any attempt to get a job at our house."

"Why?"

"He was afraid she would give us damaging information about him."

"By 'us' do you mean you and your wife?"

"I mean myself only. Mrs. Brandon is inclined to believe the best of everyone. She's a very trusting soul."

"So is Rupert," Dodd said, "or he would never have attempted the phone trick, knowing there was an extension in the bedroom."

"Trusting? Perhaps. Perhaps only stupid."

"Amateur, anyway."

"Amateur." Gill nodded vigorous agreement. "That's what he is. And that's why he'll be caught."

Dodd folded his hands and closed his eyes, like a minister about to pray for some lost souls which he strongly suspected would remain lost. "Tell me, Mr. Brandon, has Gerda Lundquist given you any damaging information about your brother-in-law? For instance, did he have a bad temper? Did he quarrel frequently with his wife? Was he a lush or a chaser?"

"No, not to my knowledge."

"What's the worst Gerda had to say about him?"

"He was—moody."

"And that's all?"

"She also said that last spring he was frequently late coming home. He claimed he was working overtime."

"At what period in the spring?"

"March, I believe she said."

"March," Dodd pointed out, "is income-tax time, and your brother-in-law is an accountant. He was lucky to get home at all."

Gill flushed. "Just whose side are you on, anyway?"

"I never take sides until both teams are out in the field and I know what game they're going to play."

"This is no game, Mr. Dodd. My sister is missing. Find her."

"I'm trying," Dodd said. "Did you bring the pictures?"

"Yes."

The pictures were in a manila envelope: two formal photographs and about a dozen large colored snapshots. In most of the snapshots Amy was smiling, but both the photographs showed her grave and self-conscious, as if she hadn't wanted to be in front of a camera at all, knowing in advance the results wouldn't satisfy anyone. *Repressed*, Dodd thought. *Anxious to please. Too anxious.*

One of the snapshots showed her sitting on a lawn with a small black dog on a leash beside her. Against the green grass the red and black plaid of the dog's leash and collar stood out distinctly.

"That's Mack?" Dodd said.

"Yes. He's a pedigreed Scottish terrier. I gave him to Amy for her birthday five years ago. She's devoted to him, too much so, in fact. He's only a dog, after all, not a child, but she takes him everywhere she goes, downtown shopping and so on. She even wanted to take him with her to Mexico City but she was afraid of a possible quarantine at the border."

"She kept him on leash?"

"Always. And always on this particular leash. You may not notice anything special about it, unless you're an expert on tartans, but this tartan is not very commonly seen. It represents the Maclachlan clan. Mack was registered with the American Kennel Club under his official name, Maclachlan's Merryheart, and Amy got the fanciful idea of having a collar, leash and sweater made up for him in the proper tartan. The set cost a hundred dollars, almost as much as the dog itself."

Gill paused to light a cigarette. The pictures of Amy, spread over Dodd's desk, smiled up at him mockingly: *All this fuss over me and my little dog. We're in New York, Gilly. We're doing all the shows. Mack's wearing the new hand-tooled leather leash I bought him in Mexico City...*

"Wherever Amy is," Gill said, "she didn't take Mack with her. His leash is still hanging in the kitchen."

"Rupert had an explanation for that. He told Gerda..."

"I know what he told Gerda, but it isn't true."

"I agree that it doesn't seem likely," Dodd said cautiously. "It's possible, though."

"If you knew Amy you wouldn't think so. She's childishly proud of Mack's tartan."

"Then where is the dog?"

"I'd give a great deal to know the answer to that."

You may have to, Dodd thought. Finding people was tough enough. Finding a Scottie that looked like a thousand other Scotties seemed impossible. There wasn't even any guarantee that the dog was still alive. He said, "Why should Kellogg have told you in the first place that Amy took the dog with her?"

"To convince me that Amy came home and went away again of her own accord."

"Is there any evidence that she did come home?"

"Rupert's word."

"No one else saw her?"

"No one, to my knowledge."

Dodd consulted his notes. "Let's see, she came back from Mexico City, allegedly, on Sunday, September the fourteenth, and left again that same night without calling anyone to say good-bye and without being seen by anyone we know of except Rupert. Right?"

"Yes."

"Have you any idea why?"

"Why she didn't call me and wasn't seen? Certainly I have an idea. She never came home. Perhaps she never even left Mexico City."

"Let's be frank, Mr. Brandon. Do you believe your sister is dead?"

Gill looked down at the smiling pictures on Dodd's desk. *Me, dead? Don't be absurd, Gilly. I'm in New York. I'm having a ball.* He said, through tight lips, "Yes. I believe he killed her."

"And his motive?"

"Money."

Dodd sighed, very faintly. If it wasn't money, it was love. Perhaps they both boiled down to the same thing, security.

"He has her power of attorney," Gill said. "He doesn't even have to wait for proof of death so he can inherit her money."

"Did your sister make a will?"

"Yes. Rupert inherits half her estate."

"Who gets the other half?"

"I do."

Dodd said nothing but his black, bushy eyebrows moved up and down his forehead. *Very interesting, Mr. Brandon. I know—and you don't know I know—that you've been living beyond your income for some time now, taking bites out of your capital to feed some pretty undernourished investments.* "It would, then, if your sister is dead, be to your advantage to prove it as quickly as possible."

"What do you mean?"

"As long as Mrs. Kellogg is simply missing, the power of attorney she gave her husband is in force. He has full control over her property, and how much will be left for you or anyone else to inherit depends entirely on his discretion. Let's assume your sister is dead. From your point of view—that is, keeping her property intact and at full value—it would be an advantage to get proof of death immediately. From his point of view, the longer the delay, the better it will be for him."

"I don't like to—to think of these things."

You've already thought of them, old boy; don't kid me. "Come now, Mr. Brandon, it's just a little game we're playing. Your sister, by the way, must have trusted Rupert completely or she would never have given him a power of attorney."

"Perhaps. But he might have applied some form of pressure to get it."

"You said he has a small but successful business of his own?"

"Yes."

"And he lives modestly?"

"There's no guarantee he intends to continue living modestly," Gill said. "That calm exterior of his might be hiding some pretty fancy and wild ideas."

"Do you believe his dismissal of Gerda Lundquist was, as he claimed, a matter of economic necessity?"

"Not unless he's been having some unusual expenses."

"Such as gambling debts?"

"Such as another woman."

"That's pure speculation on your part, is it, Mr. Brandon? Or impure, as the case may be."

"You may call it speculation. I call it simple arithmetic. Two and two add up to Miss Burton, his secretary." Gill ground out his cigarette in an overflowing ash tray advertising Luigi's Pizza House on Mason Street. "I have two secretaries, but I assure you that neither of them has a key to my back door, neither of them looks after my dog, neither of them drops in after church to clean up my house."

"It will be easy enough to check up on Miss Burton."

"Do it subtly. If she suspects anything she'll tell Rupert immediately and he'll find out I hired you. He mustn't know a thing about any of this. Surprise must be the basis of our tactics."

"*My* tactics, if you don't mind, Mr. Brandon."

"All right, yours. So long as he's caught. And punished."

Dodd leaned back in his swivel chair, interlacing his fingers. It seemed clear to him now that Brandon wanted Rupert punished more than he wanted his sister found. He shivered slightly. It was three o'clock on a sunny afternoon. It felt like midnight in the dead of winter.

He got up and shut the window, and almost immediately opened it again. He didn't like the sensation of being in a closed room with Gill Brandon. "Tell me, have you talked to your brother-in-law since the morning he gave you the letter?"

"No."

"You haven't communicated any of your suspicions to him?"

"No."

"It might clear the air if you did."

"I'm not giving him any advantage by tipping my hand."

"Are you sure you have a hand?"

"I'm sure. Nobody lies the way he's lied unless he has something to hide."

"All right," Dodd said. "Let's leave Rupert out of this for a minute. Where, to your knowledge, was your sister last seen?"

"At the hospital where she was taken after Wilma's death sent her into shock. The American-British-Corday, I believe it's called."

"And what was the name of the hotel she and her friend were staying at?"

"It was their intention to stay at the Windsor. Whether they did or not, I'm not sure. Mrs. Wyatt was very changeable, and

89

if some little thing didn't suit her she would have gone some-place else. Wherever they stayed, you can bet that it was Mrs. Wyatt's decision. My sister has never learned to stick up for her rights."

Dodd wrote: Windsor Hotel? Sept. 3. A.B.C. Hospital, Sept. 7. Then he gathered up the pictures of Amy, put them back in the manila folder and marked it A. KELLOGG. "I'm going to send a couple of these down to a friend of mine in Mexico City."

"Why?"

"He might be willing, for a fee, to do some investigating. That's where the trouble seems to have started. Let's get an objective report, since you're reluctant to believe anything your brother-in-law says."

"Who is this friend?"

"A retired cop from L.A. called Fowler. He's good. And expensive."

"How expensive?"

"I can't give you an exact figure."

Gill took an unmarked envelope out of his pocket and put it on Dodd's desk. "There's five hundred in cash. Is that sufficient for the time being?"

"That depends."

"On what?"

"On how much bribe money my friend's going to need."

"Bribe money? Whom does he have to bribe?"

"In Mexico," Dodd said dryly, "practically everyone."

10

Thursday was Pat Burton's dancing night at the Kent Academy. She didn't bother going home after work. She took her dancing equipment to the office with her—a pair of transparent plastic shoes with three-inch heels and a bottle of strongly scented cologne because the Academy always had a rancid smell like an unventilated school gymnasium. The cologne was, therefore, an asset if not a necessity; the Cinderella shoes were not. They impeded Miss Burton's progress. After eleven months of lessons (Learn to Dance the First Night) she was still having considerable trouble with the mambo, and her tango included numerous extracurricular totters which were the despair of the instructor. "Miss Burton, save your wiggles for the cha-cha-cha. Keep your *balance.*" "I can do it perfectly well at home in my bare feet." "Since when do we teach the tango so people can do it at home in their bare feet?"

It didn't matter very much anyway because no one invited Miss Burton out mambaing or tangoing. Her infrequent dates preferred less sophisticated or less strenuous entertainment. She continued going to the weekly class, however. It represented to her, as well as to the majority of the others, a social rather than an instructive evening.

The class was already in progress when Miss Burton arrived. One of her frequent partners, an elderly retired lawyer, a widower named Jacobson, waved to her out of a fast rhumba and Miss Burton waved back, thinking, *one of these days he's going to drop dead right on the floor. I just hope it's not me he's dancing with when it happens.*

The instructor screamed over the music at no one in particular, "Don't sway your hips! Forget about your hips! If your feet are doing the right thing your hips will do the right thing. Do I make myself *heard*?"

He made himself heard but hips refused to be forgotten.

Miss Burton tapped her foot and surveyed the room from the doorway. Not many spectators tonight. A woman with a little girl. A pair of teen-agers, a boy and a girl, with matching shirts and matching expressions of boredom. A middle-aged woman wearing a pound of pearls. And, standing right next to Miss Burton herself, a man with bushy gray hair that seemed to emphasize the youthful alertness of his face. He looked as though he had wandered into the place by mistake, but now that he was there he was determined to get the most out of it.

He said, with a slight frown, "I don't understand the business about not swaying your hips. That's a rhumba they're doing, isn't it?"

"Yes."

"I thought in a rhumba you were supposed to sway your hips."

Miss Burton smiled. "You're new here, aren't you?"

"Yes. My first time."

"Are you going to be in the class?"

"I guess so," the man said, sounding rather pained. "I guess I have to."

"Why? There's no law about it."

"Well, you see I won a scholarship. I can't very well waste it."

"What kind of scholarship?"

"There was this advertisement in the paper showing pictures of people doing various kinds of dances. If you identified the dances correctly you were given a scholarship, thirty dollars' worth of free lessons. I won. I can't understand it exactly," he added. "I mean, there are a lot of people know more about dancing than I do, thousands of them. But I won."

Miss Burton didn't want to hurt his feelings but she didn't want him to be taken in, either. He was so naïve and earnest, a little bit like Mr. Kellogg. "I'm sure you could win lots of *real* contests if you put your mind to it."

"This one wasn't real?"

"No. Everybody won. It was just a come-on so the Kent Academy could get the names of people who are interested in dancing."

"But I'm not interested in dancing. I'm just interested in contests."

Miss Burton whooped with laughter. "Oh dear. That's a good joke on the Academy. What other kind of contests do you go in for?"

"Any kind. Also tests. I buy all the magazines and do the tests, like, for instance, 'Would You Make a Good Engineer?', or 'What Is Your Social I.Q.?', or 'Can You Qualify as a Quiz Contestant?' Things like that. I do pretty well in them." He added with a sigh: "I guess they're rigged too, like this here contest."

"Oh, I don't believe that," Miss Burton said loyally. "Maybe you really would make a good engineer."

"I hope so. I do some engineering occasionally."

"What kind of engineering?"

"It's classified."

"You mean, like secret missiles and things?"

"That's close enough," he replied. "What do you do?"

"Me? Oh, I'm just a secretary. I work for Rupert Kellogg. He's an accountant."

"I've heard of him." *Too often*, he thought. *Much too often*.

"He's the best accountant in town. The best boss too."

"You don't say."

"Other bosses I've had used to get their mean days. Mr. Kellogg never has a mean day."

"I bet children and dogs take to him right off the bat."

"Maybe you mean that as a joke, but it's absolutely true. Mr. Kellogg's crazy about animals. You know what he told me once? He told me he didn't really like being an accountant, he wanted to open a pet store."

"Why doesn't he?"

"His wife comes from a ritzy family. They wouldn't approve, I guess."

Old Mr. Jacobson, the retired lawyer, rhumbaed past, wriggling like a nervous snake, and gave Miss Burton a grin and a wink. His face was as moist and red as a sliced beet.

"He seems to be having a fine time," the man said.

"That's Mr. Jacobson. He knows all the dances perfectly, only he can't keep time."

"He's certainly caught the spirit of the thing anyway."

"I'll say. One of these days he's going to drop dead right on this very floor. It kind of spoils my evening thinking about it."

The music ended, and the instructor announced in a tired shriek that the next number would be a change of pace, the slicker waltz, and would the men kindly remember that a good strong lead was necessary in this one, especially at the turns?

Mr. Jacobson sped in Miss Burton's direction. Miss Burton turned red and whispered an anguished "Oh dear." But she didn't have enough nerve, or presence of mind, to head for the powder room. So she stood her ground and uttered a short, quiet prayer: *Don't let this be the night.*

Mr. Jacobson was as merry as Old King Cole. "Come on, Miss B. Let's have at it!"

"Oh, don't you think you'd better rest a bit?"

"Nonsense. I have the whole week to rest. Thursday's my night to shake a leg."

"Yes. Well."

Miss Burton surrendered reluctantly to Mr. Jacobson's bony arms and good strong lead. This might be, could very well be, Mr. Jacobson's last dance. The least she could do was to make it as pleasant as possible for him by trying to follow him properly, and at the same time watch his face for any telltale signs of the end approaching. She wasn't sure what the signs would be, and the strain of looking up at him gave her a crick in the neck.

"You're not concentrating tonight, Miss B."

"Oh yes, I am," Miss Burton said grimly.

"Loosen up a little. Relax. Enjoy yourself. This is supposed to be fun."

"Yes."

"What's the matter, something on your mind?"

"Just—the usual."

"Get it off. Tell someone. Tell me."

"Oh, dear me, no," Miss Burton said hastily. "Haven't we been having lovely weather this fall? Of course, we can't expect you—it to last."

Mr. Jacobson didn't catch the error because the instructor had raised his voice again. "This is ballroom dancing. This is not real life. In real life women don't like to be pushed around. In ballroom dancing they expect to be, they want to be, they have to be! So lead, gentlemen! You're not zombies! Lead!"

"You have a real good lead," Miss Burton said.

"And you have a mighty fine follow," Mr. Jacobson replied gallantly.

"No, I haven't, not really. I do all the dances much better at home in my bare feet. I get shook up when people watch me."

"Such as the man at the door?"

"Oh dear, is he watching me? My goodness."

"Watching people is his business, or part of it."

"What do you mean?"

"He's a private detective named Dodd. I used to see him hanging around the Hall of Justice. He had a lot of nicknames in those days, the least objectionable of which was Fingers, because he had a finger in every pie."

"It must be a case of mistaken identity," Miss Burton said in a high, tight voice. "He told me he was an engineer. He's doing secret work."

Mr. Jacobson chuckled. "On whom?"

"He's—he's here because he won a scholarship."

"Don't you believe it. That's Dodd. And he's here because he wants information from someone."

"Who?"

"Well, whom was he talking to?"

"Me," Miss Burton said, and both her heart and her feet missed a beat.

Dodd caught the startled look she threw him and knew that Jacobson had told her who he was. He thought, *I should have recognized Jacobson sooner, but he's lost fifty pounds. Well, there's no harm done. Let Miss Burton get fussed up. She might tell me more of the truth by lying.*

"But I don't have any information," Miss Burton insisted.

Mr. Jacobson winked. "Ah, don't you now."

"I really don't. Maybe Mr. Dodd is here after somebody else. That Mr. Lessups who enrolled last week, he looks like a crook."

"Don't we all. Now, Miss B., you're tightening up again. Relax."

"How can I, with a policeman staring at me like that?"

"He's not a policeman. He's a private detective."

"It's the same thing for my money."

"Then your money's wrong. Mr. Dodd has no authority whatever. You don't have to say a word to him. Tell him to go roll his hoop."

"I can't."

"And why not?"

"I—I'd kind of like to find out what he's doing here."

"In brief, your curiosity is greater than your fear. Ah, women. Well, the best of luck, my dear. And if you can't be good, be careful."

Dodd was waiting for her at the doorway. When she tried to pass him he put out his hand to stop her. "I gather Mr. Jacobson has introduced me? That's all right. I intended to do it myself eventually. Would you like to go someplace for a cup of coffee?"

"I definitely would not."

"That's honest anyway. Are you honest about everything, Miss Burton?"

"I don't go around telling people I'm an engineer."

"I told you I did some engineering. I do."

"Well, you're not going to do any engineering on me," Miss Burton said coldly. "You have no authority to question me about anything."

"That's what Jacobson told you?"

"Yes and he's a lawyer and he should know."

"Of course," Dodd agreed. "What interests me is, why are you so afraid of questions? I've learned quite a lot about you, Miss Burton, and it seems to me you have nothing to hide or be ashamed of."

"What do you mean you learned quite a lot about me? How? Why?"

"Hold on a minute. You're asking me questions. You haven't any authority to do that, have you?"

"I…"

"You see, this thing works both ways. I have no authority, you have no authority. Nobody asks questions, nobody gets any answers. Not an ideal way to run things, is it? Now let's sit down and have a reasonable talk. How about it?"

"Maybe I'd better ask Mr. Jacobson first."

"You haven't been accused of any crime. You don't need a lawyer."

Miss Burton sat down. "O.K., what do you want?"

"I'm looking for a missing person. I thought you might be able to help."

"How can I help? I don't even know any missing person."

"Yes, you do," Dodd said.

11

It was cold and late, and ghosts of fog were prowling the streets of the city, but Miss Burton didn't notice the time or the weather. She hurried along the sidewalk, propelled by fright, guided by instinct. Her handbag, containing the dancing shoes and the bottle of cologne, hung heavy from her shoulder and knocked against one hip as she moved.

From his parked car Dodd saw her turn the corner toward Market Street. He made no attempt to follow her since he was sure of her intention. He had planted the intention himself, deliberately, and watched it grow in her transparent eyes the way a botanist watches a seed grow between two layers of glass.

With a final flip of her yellow coat Miss Burton disappeared around the corner of Woolworth's and Dodd was left pondering some second and third thoughts about the advisability of dragging her into the case. She was a nice girl. He didn't like to use her, but business was business. If Rupert Kellogg was innocent of any wrongdoing, he deserved to be warned about Brandon's suspicions and operations. If he was guilty, a warning might jolt him into action. So far he'd done nothing but sit tight and tell stories, some thin, some tall. Brandon himself was certainly not admitting the whole truth. No living woman could be as flawless as Amy.

Dodd turned on the ignition of the little Volkswagen. He was tired and depressed. For the first time since entering the case he had the feeling that Brandon might be right about his sister. Wherever and whenever Amy was found, she wouldn't be found alive.

The house was dark. Miss Burton had never seen it at night, wrapped in fog, and she was not sure it was the right place until she went up on the veranda and saw the bronze nameplate on the door, Rupert J. Kellogg. A few hours ago the sight of the name would have given her a pleasant little thrill. Now it seemed strange, without any relation to the man who owned it. She pressed the door chime and waited, shivering with cold and fear and self- doubt. *What am, I doing here? What will I say to him? How can I act calm as if nothing had happened, as if Dodd had never told me those terrible things?*

Take care of yourself, Dodd had said. *A woman has disappeared, don't make it two.*

She turned her head quickly and peered through the fog at the street, hoping for a moment that Dodd had followed her. But there were no cars parked along the curb, and no one was walking along the street or waiting under a lamppost. She was alone. She could enter this house and never be seen again and no one would be able to say, "Yes, I noticed her, a small woman in a yellow coat, shortly after eleven o'clock—she went in and never came out…"

The hall light splashed through the window and she reared back as if someone had thrown it at her like acid. Panting, she leaned against a pillar and watched the door slowly open.

"Why, Miss Burton," Rupert said. "What are you doing here?"

"I—I don't—know."

"Is anything the matter?"

"Ev—everything."

"You haven't been drinking, have you?"

"No. I never drink. I'm a M-M-Methodist."

"Well, that's very interesting," he said wearily, "but I hope you didn't come all the way out here at this time of night to tell me you're a Methodist."

She pressed against the pillar, her teeth chattering like castanets. She wanted to run away but she was both afraid for him and afraid of him, and the double fear immobilized her.

"Miss Burton?"

"I—I was just passing by and I thought I'd—drop in and say hello. I didn't realize how—late it was. I'm sorry to have bothered you. I'd—better be going."

"You'd better not be going," he said sharply. "You'd better be coming in and telling me about it."

"About—what?"

"Whatever it is that's making you act like this." He opened the door wider, and waited. "Come on."

"I can't. It wouldn't be proper."

"All right, I'll call you a cab."

"No! I mean, I don't want a cab."

"You can't stand here all night, can you?"

She shook her head and her limp, blond curls fell over her eyes so that she looked like a little old lady peering out at him through a lace curtain. He wondered what was going on behind the lace curtain.

He said, "You're cold."

"I know."

"You'd better come inside and get warm."

"Yes. All right."

He closed the door behind her and led her down the hall to the den. An unscreened fire was burning in the grate, its flames reflected in the silver box on the coffee table. He saw her glance at the box, but briefly and without interest. There was no danger here. She couldn't possibly know anything about the box.

"Sit down, Miss Burton."

"Thank you."

"Now, what's troubling you?"

"I—well, I went to dancing class tonight at the Kent Academy. I always do on Thursdays. Not that I'm a good dancer or anything, it's just a way of passing time and meeting people. Usually the people are O.K., nothing special but O.K. Nothing sneaky about them, I mean. If you meet someone there and he says he's an engineer, that's what he is, an engineer. So you're not suspicious, I mean."

She hadn't intended to tell him about the dancing classes for fear he would laugh at her, but the words just came tumbling out of her mouth like blown bubbles. He didn't laugh at her, though. He seemed very grave and interested.

"Go on, Miss Burton."

"Well, tonight I met this man. He's a terrible man. He said things, suggested things."

"I'm sure you know how to deal with improper suggestions, Miss Burton."

She flushed and looked down at her hands. "They weren't suggestions like the kind you mean. They were about you. And Mrs. Kellogg."

"Who was the man?"

"His name's Dodd. He's a private detective. Oh, he didn't let on he was a private detective. He tried to palm himself off as a new student, but I have this friend at the Academy, he's a lawyer…"

"What did this man Dodd say about Mrs. Kellogg?"

"That she was missing. Under mysterious circumstances."

"She is not missing. She is in New York."

"I told him that. But he just smiled—he has the nastiest smile, like a camel's—and said New York was a big place with a lot of people in it but he didn't think one of them was Mrs. Kellogg." Before the warmth of the fire Miss Burton's suspicions of Rupert were evaporating like fog under the heat of the sun. "If I were you I'd sue him for slander. It's a free country but people can't go around saying anything in their heads when it does harm to other people."

"Well, don't get excited."

"I'm not excited. I'm good and mad. I said to him, 'Listen, you keyhole cop. Mr. Kellogg's the finest man in this city, and if Mrs. Kellogg is missing it's not his fault, it's hers, and why don't you put the blame on the right person?' And he said, as a matter of fact, he'd been thinking along those same lines himself."

She waited, expecting his approval and his gratitude for her support. What she had no reason to expect was his quiet, malevolent whisper: "You imbecile."

Her face crumpled under the surprise attack. "What—what did I do?"

"What didn't you do!"

"But I was only sticking up for you, I was only trying…"

"You tried. All right. Let's leave it like that."

"I don't understand," she wailed. "What did I say wrong?"

"Probably everything." He went over to the window, lengthening the time and space between them so that he might have a chance to regain control of himself, and, consequently, of her. He had no doubt of her loyalty. But what was loyalty? Would it break under pressure, bend under heat? How much of the truth would it take?

He could see her reflection in the window, her eyes wide with bewilderment and pain: *What did I do?* She looked young and simple. He knew she was neither.

"I'm sorry, Miss Burton," he said, addressing her reflection because it was easier to lie to a reflection. "I had no right to speak roughly to you."

"You did so have a right," she said faintly. "If I did something wrong, even if I didn't mean to, you've got a perfect right to check me up. Only I still don't understand just what I…"

"You will, someday. For the moment we'd better both forget it."

"But how can I stop doing something if I don't know what I did?"

He closed his eyes for a moment. He was too weary to talk, to think, to plan, but he realized that he couldn't allow her to leave without some explanation or instruction. It would be all right if she remained as she was now, contrite, meek, low in energy. But what of the difference in her after a night's rest, a time to think, a good breakfast?

He could visualize her bouncing into the office in the morning (with some of the loyalty rubbed off like fuzz off a peach) and greeting Borowitz with the news: "Guess what, Borowitz? Last night I met a real private detective and he was asking me all kinds of questions about the boss's wife disappearing." And Borowitz, who was by nature and habit a gossip, would relay it to his girlfriend, and the girlfriend to her family, and within days it would cover the city, spread by mouth like a morbid virus. The initial carrier must be stopped. It no longer mattered how.

"Miss Burton, I have great faith in your discretion, as well as your loyalty and good will. I depend on them." He despised the false tone, the false words. They wouldn't even have fooled the little dog Mack, but Miss Burton was breathing them in like oxygen. "I am going to take you into my confidence, knowing you'll respect it."

"Oh, I will. My goodness, I certainly will."

"My wife *is* missing, in the sense that I'm not sure where she is. I've told people she is in New York because I had a letter from her postmarked New York and because I have to tell them something."

"Why doesn't she let you know where she is?"

"It was part of our agreement before she left. For lack of a better term, call it a trial separation. We were to let each other strictly alone for a period of time. Unfortunately, my brother-in-law, Mr. Brandon, doesn't believe in letting anyone alone. He hired a private detective to look for Amy. Well, I hope he finds her, not for her sake or mine, but for Mr. Brandon's. He's making a terrible fool of himself. His wife knows it and has tried to stop him. Failing that, she came and told me all about it."

"Was that the day she came to the office all dressed up?"

Rupert nodded. "Somewhere along the line Mr. Brandon picked up the idea that I wanted to get rid of my wife because I'm interested in another woman." He turned to face her. She was leaning forward in the chair, tense and excited, like a child listening to a fairy tale. "Do you know who the woman is, Miss Burton?"

"Why, no. Why, my goodness…"

"You."

Her mouth fell open so that he could see the silver fillings in her bottom row of teeth. *Silver,* he thought. *Silver box. I must get rid of the silver box. First, I must get rid of her.*

He said, patiently, sympathetically, "I'm sorry this comes as a shock to you, Miss Burton. It did to me, too."

She had dropped back into the chair, pale and limp. "That—that awful man. To say, even to *think,* such a terrible thing—trying to ruin my good name…"

"Not yours. Mine."

"And all these years I've been a good Methodist, never even thinking about carnal things!" But even as she spoke the words, she knew they were not true. Rupert popped up too often in her mind, in her dreams, as father, as son, as lover. Perhaps he knew. Perhaps he could read it in her eyes. She covered her face with her hands and repeated in a high muffled voice, "Always a g-g-good Methodist."

"Of course. Of course you are."

"I—just because I touch up my hair. Nothing in the Bible says you can't change the color of your hair. I went to the minister and asked him. I always ask the minister for advice when I'm worried."

He looked down at her stonily, without compassion, seeing her not as a woman but as a threat, an unexploded bomb whose firing pin had to be removed with the most meticulous care. "Are you worried now, Miss Burton?"

"Worried to death."

"Does that mean you intend to talk this over with your minister?"

"I don't know. He's a very wise..."

"This is a delicate situation, Miss Burton. Undoubtedly your minister is a man of wisdom and good will, but are you sure you want still another person to hear the rumor?"

"What do you mean, *still another?*"

"Mrs. Brandon knows. And the detective, Dodd. Gerda Lundquist too, probably, since she's now working for the Brandons."

"They can't know anything," Miss Burton said shrilly. "There's nothing to know. It's just a vicious rumor. I'll deny it."

"Can you?"

"Yes, I can. There isn't a word of truth in it!"

"Not one word?"

She shook her head back and forth in silent pain.

"Miss Burton, suppose I told you there is some truth in it, that it's not just a rumor?"

"No. No! Don't tell me anything!"

"All right."

He watched the tears slither out between her fingers and roll down her skinny wrists. *She won't explode now,* he thought. *She'll just make a lot of noise and fizzle out.*

She was a crying woman, not a bomb any more. He took a long deep breath and crossed the room toward her.

"Miss Burton—Pat."

"Don't come near me! Don't tell me anything!"

"I said I wouldn't. But you'd better stop crying now. Your eyes swell up when you cry."

"How—how do you know?"

"I remember when you came to work after your mother's funeral. Your eyelids were like blisters, and they stayed that way all day. You looked very funny."

Slowly she took her hands away from her face. He was smiling down at her, so gently and affectionately that her heart gave a sudden thrust against her chest wall like the kick of a fetus.

He said, "You don't want Borowitz suspecting you've had an emotional upset. If he sees that you've been crying he'll ask questions. You have no answers."

"I have—no answers."

"You're tired. Sit there quietly for a minute while I call a cab for you. Will you?"

"Yes."

"And no more tears?"

"No."

He called the cab from the phone in the kitchen, remembering the last time he'd called one, on a Sunday evening almost three weeks previously. He'd put in the order for a cab, and then three minutes later, according to plan, he'd canceled it. The cab company would have a record of the address and the cancellation. He didn't know how long the company would keep such a record. Long enough, he hoped, for Dodd to find out about it; so far he was finding all the wrong things, like a retriever bringing back the decoys instead of the dead ducks. No, it was the other way around....

When he returned, Miss Burton had stopped crying but she still looked moist and disheveled.

"You'd better straighten up a bit," he said. "You know where the bathrooms are."

She blushed at the word, which seemed suddenly intimate and full of meaning.

"We don't want the cab driver getting curious about your appearance," he added. "You'll be picked up, by the way, at the northwest corner of Cabrillo in ten minutes. I thought it would be more discreet than having him come here. Incidentally, discreet is a good word for you to remember."

"I never ever had to be discreet before," she said painfully. "I never ever had anything to hide before."

"Have you now?"

"I—I don't—know."

"If you don't know, you'd better act on the assumption that you have."

"I feel so confused."

"Try not to let it show."

"How can I help it? How can I go to the office tomorrow morning like nothing has happened?"

"You've got to," he said. "You have no choice."

"I can quit. Maybe under the circumstances, it would be better if I quit."

"Do you realize what will happen if you do? Mr. Brandon will immediately assume that I'm setting you up in a love nest, with my wife's money."

She shrank inside the yellow coat as if it were a hiding shell, a protection from the terrible intimacy of such words as *love nest*.

"I'm trying to help you, Miss Burton. But you have to help yourself too. And me. We're in this together."

"No," she whispered. "We're not. We're not in anything together. I haven't done anything, said anything. I'm innocent. I'm *innocent!*"

"I know you are."

"But I've got to prove it. How can I prove it?"

"By keeping control of yourself. Don't discuss me or my personal affairs with anyone. Don't answer questions, don't volunteer information."

"Those are all *don'ts*. What can I *do*?"

"The best thing would be to hurry up and get out of here. Now go and wash your face and comb your hair." The words were brusque but he spoke them in a kindly, almost paternal tone, and she reacted like an obedient child.

In the bathroom off the kitchen she washed her face and dried it on the only towel hanging on the rack. She knew it must be Rupert's towel and when she pressed it against her forehead and her hot cheeks she wanted to cry again, just stand there for a long time and cry.

He was waiting for her in the kitchen, wearing his topcoat and a fedora. His skin looked gray under the fluorescent lights. "I'll walk you to the corner."

"No. You must be tired. You should go to bed."

"I don't want you walking along a city street alone at midnight."

"Is it midnight?"

"Later than that."

Outside, the fog was dripping from the eaves like rain. They walked side by side, as far apart as they could get on the narrow sidewalk, self-consciously avoiding personal contact. But the contact was there, invisibly bridging the space between them. Miss Burton could feel it as she had felt it in the bathroom, pressing Rupert's towel against her face. She was exquisitely aware of every movement he made, every breath he took, the stride of his long legs, the swing of his arms, the sighs that seemed to be words which mustn't be said. *What words,* she thought, *and do I want to hear them?*

She spoke to hide her thoughts. "It's so—quiet."

"Yes."

"Funny, I feel so noisy inside."

"Noisy in what way?"

"Gongs. Gongs are clanking."

He smiled slightly. "I've never heard gongs. Thunder, though. Lots of that."

"I guess everybody has their own personal noise inside."

"I guess they do," he said. "Your cab's waiting."

"I see it."

"Here's five dollars to cover your fare."

She felt that by accepting the money she was accepting more than her taxi fare, but she didn't argue, didn't even hesitate. He put the five-dollar bill in her outstretched hand. It was the only physical contact they'd had all evening.

He returned to the house and, for the dozenth time that day, he reread the letter that had accompanied the silver box.

Dear Rupert:

I wish to thank you and Amy for the beautiful wreath, and you for the note of condolence. The funeral was very quiet, and though Wilma would have called it oversentimental, we found it satisfying. Perhaps, as Wilma always claimed, funerals are barbaric affairs, but they are a custom and a convention, and in times of stress we lean on custom and convention.

I hope that Amy has recovered from the shock by this time. It was unfortunate that she had to be a witness, or that anyone had to be. But Wilma may have planned it that way—she could never do anything in private, there always had to be an audience, whether it was an applauding one or a hissing one. Her other attempt at suicide, after her first divorce, was undertaken in the bathroom of a friend's house while a large party was going on. None of us there felt we could have prevented what happened, so Amy must not feel that she could have prevented it…

Rupert remembered the occasion well. Amy had been at Lake Tahoe with the Brandons at the time, so he had gone alone to the hospital to see Wilma. Without makeup, and wearing a regulation gown, she looked pale and haggard.

"Wilma?"

"Fancy meeting you here. Sit down and make yourself comfortable. If anyone can be comfortable in this stinking hole."

"What in God's name made you do it, Wilma?"

"Such a question."

"I'm asking it."

"O.K., I was bored. All those silly people chattering and laughing. I saw the pills in the medicine cabinet and took them. Have you ever had your stomach pumped out? It's quite an experience."

"I think you'd better go and see a psychiatrist."

"I've been seeing one for the past two weeks. He's very cute. He has the curliest eyelashes. I sit and look at his eyelashes for fifty minutes three times a week. It's fascinating. I may get a crush on him. On the other hand I may get bored. There's not a hell of a lot to eyelashes."

"You've got to take this seriously."

"I'm tired, pal. Get out, will you?"

In less than two months Wilma became bored with the psychiatrist's eyelashes and quit seeing him.

Rupert returned to the letter.

… I could talk about Wilma for hours at a time—and often have—but I never seem to reach any clearer understanding of her. What a pity that all her drive and energy wasn't channeled into constructive outlets. It would have been far better if she'd had to go out and support herself instead of living on alimony checks. We have not been able, by the way, to find out where Wilma's husband, Robert Wyatt, is to tell him about Wilma's death. He won't be very interested anyway, except that it will save him money.

You're probably wondering about the silver box. It was among Wilma's things that were sent on to me from Mexico City. It must have been damaged in transit, but it is still a handsome piece of work. Earl and I assumed, from the monogram inside the lid, that she intended it as a gift for you. She always spoke of you with deep affection, and I know how patient you and Amy have been with what Earl called Wilma's "shenanigans." Please keep the box in memory of her.

Give our best regards to Amy and thank you again for the beautiful wreath. Yellow roses were always Wilma's favorite. How thoughtful of you to remember.

Sincerely,

RUTH SULLIVAN.

Yellow roses.

"I hope," Wilma had said once, "that when I die someone will send me yellow roses. How about it, Rupert?"

"All right. If I'm still around."

"Is that a promise?"

"Certainly."

"Promises to dead people are easy to break. When I think of all the promises I made to my parents—if I've kept any of them it's sheer accident. So forget the whole thing, will you?"

"I don't think," Amy had said primly, "that people ought to talk about their own funerals…"

He tossed the letter and its envelope into the fire. Then he picked up the silver box hesitantly, as if he didn't want to touch it. It looked like a coffin. But not Wilma's coffin. The initials on the lid were his own.

He went out to the garage, holding the box under his topcoat.

Half an hour later, as he approached the middle of Golden Gate Bridge, he threw the little silver coffin over the guard rail. It sank first into the fog, then into the sea.

12

The runways of International Airport were steaming under the heat of a surprise sun, and planes that had been grounded overnight were taking off in all directions as fast as space could be cleared for them. Inside the glass walls the loudspeaker, like an invisible tyrant, gave out constant orders to its subjects: "Pan American, flight 509 for Hawaii, now boarding at Gate Seven... Mr. Paul Mitchell, report to United Air Lines, Mr. Paul Mitchell... Trans World Airlines flight 703 to Chicago and New York has been delayed half an hour... Do not attempt to board planes before your flight number has been announced... Gate Seven is now open for Pan American flight 509 to Hawaii... Mrs. James Swartz, repeat, Mrs. James Swartz, your ticket has not been validated for Dallas, Texas. Report immediately to the United Air Lines desk... Gate Ten is now open for flight 314 to Seattle..."

Behind the Western Air Lines counter, a young pink-faced man in horn-rimmed spectacles was doing some paper work behind a nameplate that identified him as Charles E. Smith.

When Dodd approached, the young man said, without looking up, "Can I do anything for you?"

"I'd like a ticket to the moon."

"What in... Oh, it's you. Dodd. Somebody been murdered?"

"Yeah," Dodd said pleasantly. "Your whole family, including cousin Mabel, has been wiped out by a mad bomber."

"I confess."

"Good boy."

"So what else is new?"

"I'm in the market for some information, Smitty."

"I'm listening."

"On Sunday night, September the fourteenth, a man and wife supposedly landed here after a flight from Mexico City. What I want to know is, did they both get off the plane, did one of them, did either of them?"

"That sounds simple enough," Smitty said. "But it isn't."

"You keep records, don't you?"

"Sure, we keep records. We have the names of every person who's boarded any of our planes for the last two years."

Dodd looked impatient. "Well?"

"I said *boarded*. We're not in business for our health. We collect the fares and get the passengers on board. Where they get off is not our concern."

"You mean if I bought a ticket to New York and got off at Chicago instead, no one would notice the difference?"

"It wouldn't be part of our records," Smitty said. "But someone might notice the difference."

"Such as?"

"A member of the crew. One of the stewardesses, for instance, might recall you particularly because you tried to get fresh or drank three martinis before dinner instead of one. Or the radio operator, the co-pilot, the pilot—they all take trips to the head and sometimes they stop and chat with the passengers."

"Do you keep records of the crew on each flight?"

"The dispatch clerk does."

"How about looking up September the fourteenth. Better check the thirteenth, too."

Smith took off his spectacles and rubbed his eyes. "What kind of business are you on, Dodd?"

"It's never clean."

"I know that, but what's involved?"

"Love, hate, money, take your choice."

"I'll take money," Smitty said blandly.

"Are you implying that you'd accept a bribe? This is a shock to me, son, a truly terrible sh—"

"Wait in the coffee shop. I get off duty in fifteen minutes."

The coffee shop was crowded to the doors. It was easy enough to spot the people who were waiting for their planes. They ate with anxious haste, one eye on the clock, one ear on the loudspeaker. The women fussed with their hats and handbags, the men rechecked their tickets. They looked tense and irritable. Dodd wondered where all the happy travelers were that he saw in the vacation ads.

He jostled for a place at the counter and ordered coffee and a Danish pastry. While he ate he eavesdropped on the conversation of the two middle-aged women beside him who were embarking on a trip to Dallas.

"I've got this feeling I forgot something. I just *know…*"

"The gas. Did you remember to turn off the gas?"

"I'm sure I did. I *think* I did. Oh, dear!"

"You brought the Dramamine, I hope."

"Here it is. Not that it will do any good. I feel sick already."

"Imagine the nerve of them making me weigh my purse along with my luggage just because it's a little oversize."

"Even if I didn't turn off the gas the house wouldn't blow up, would it?"

"Take the Dramamine. It will quiet your nerves."

When they left, Dodd silently wished them *bon voyage* and put his topcoat over one of the vacant stools to save it for Smitty.

He was on his second cup of coffee when Smitty came in. "Done?"

"Done," Smitty said. "Saturday, September thirteen. Pilot Robert Forbes, lives in San Carlos but now in flight. Co-pilot James Billings, Sausalito, now off duty. Radio operator Joe Mazzino, Daly City, now on sick leave. Three stewardesses. Two of them, Ann Mackay and Maria Fernandez, are now in flight. The third, Betty deWitt, turned out to be married and was fired last week. Her husband's Bert Reiner, a jet pilot attached to Moffett Field and they live in Mountain View down the Peninsula. Mrs. Reiner's your girl, if you can get to her."

"How come?"

"She was the only one of the crew on both flights, the thirteenth and fourteenth, taking the place of another girl who was ill. The trouble is, Betty might not want to cooperate. She was sore as hell when they found out she was married and gave her the sack."

"I'll try my luck anyway. Thanks, Smitty. You're a model of efficiency."

"Don't applaud," Smitty said. "Just pay."

Dodd gave him ten dollars.

"Jesus, you're a cheapskate, Dodd."

"It took you fifteen minutes to get the information. That's forty bucks an hour. Where else could you make forty bucks an hour? See you later, Smitty."

He took the Bayshore Freeway back to town. When he reached his office his secretary, Lorraine, was on the phone and he knew from the sour expression on her face that she didn't like the assignment he'd given her.

"I see… Yes, Mr. Kellogg must have given me the name of the wrong kennels. Sorry to have bothered you."

She hung up, crossed out another number on the scratch pad, and immediately began dialing again.

Dodd reached over and broke the connection. "Aren't we speaking to each other this morning?"

"I have to save my voice for all these lies I'm telling."

"Any luck so far?"

"No. And I can feel an attack of laryngitis coming on."

"Until it arrives, keep phoning." Dodd knew better than to sympathize with Lorraine's ailments, which were numerous and varied enough to fill a medical textbook. "Any mail?"

"The letter came you were waiting for from Mr. Fowler in Mexico City. Special delivery. I left it on your desk."

Lorraine took a cough drop, parked it expertly inside her left cheek and began dialing again. "I am calling about Mr. Kellogg's Scottie…"

Dodd opened his letter. It was typewritten in the uneven hunt-and-peck style Fowler had used when he was a sergeant on the Los Angeles police force, and bore no date, return address or salutation.

Good to hear your voice again, you old sinner. But what's all the hurry and excitement about anyway? Everything at this end seems on the up and up.

Mrs. Kellogg was released from the A.B.C. Hospital on September twelve. I talked to the interne working on the ward she'd been in. He was reluctant, twenty-five bucks worth reluctant, but he admitted that the authorities weren't anxious to have Mrs. Kellogg leave so soon and gave their permission only when Kellogg offered to hire a nurse to accompany his wife on the trip home. According to the interne, there was considerable disagreement among the doctors about the severity of Mrs. Kellogg's concussion. Concussions can't be measured exactly even by an electro-encephalogram test,

118

which Mrs. Kellogg refused to submit to when she learned it involved needles inserted in the scalp. Personally, I can't see where Mrs. Kellogg's fear of needles fits into anything, but you wanted me to give you every single detail, so hang on. The interne's diploma is still wet, so naturally he knew all about concussions. He read it to me out of a book: the severity of a concussion can be judged by the degree of retrograde and anterograde amnesia involved. Ain't it the truth?

On the day of Mrs. Kellogg's release she and her husband returned to the Windsor Hotel. From there he put in a call to a Mr. Johnson at the American Embassy. Telephoning in this country is an art, not a science, and the switchboard operators have the temperament of opera stars. The wrong words, the wrong tone, and the *telefonista* gets her wires crossed. Apparently, Kellogg used the wrong tone. There was a lot of trouble about the call, which is how I happened to find out about it from the *telefonista* herself. I went over to the Embassy and talked to Johnson. It turned out that he was the man who'd broken the news of the affair to Kellogg and offered his services when Kellogg came down here.

Kellogg's request was simple enough. He wanted the name of a reputable lawyer who specialized in civil matters. Johnson sent him to Ramon Jiminez. Jiminez is a substantial citizen, active in politics, as well as a smart lawyer. He refused to give me any information. But when I told him I already had the information and merely wanted a confirmation or denial, he admitted that he had executed a power of attorney giving Kellogg control of his wife's affairs, financial and otherwise. Everything was legal and aboveboard. At the mere mention of the word coercion, he blew his stack (in a nice, quiet way, of course) and asked me to leave his office. My own feeling is that there can't have been any coercion involved or Jiminez wouldn't have touched the thing with a ten-foot pole. Why should he risk his reputation for the peanuts Kellogg could afford to pay? (I'm assuming that your statement about Kellogg's finances is accurate.)

Now, about the other matters you wanted me to check. No official hearing, like our American coroner's inquest, was held concerning Mrs. Wyatt's death, but some dozen eyewitnesses gave depositions to the police. The ground witnesses, i.e., those passing on the *avenida,* must be discounted, their stories were so contradictory. A combination of excitement, darkness, superstition and religious awe doesn't make for accurate observation. Mrs. Kellogg's account of the tragedy agreed substantially with that of the chambermaid, Consuela Gonzales, who for reasons known only to herself was spending the night in a nearby broom closet and heard Mrs. Kellogg screaming. She rushed into the room. Mrs. Wyatt had already flung herself over the balcony and Mrs. Kellogg was lying on the floor in a dead faint. I tried to contact Miss Gonzales at the hotel but she was fired for stealing from the guests and being insolent to the manager. The bartender, while not a witness to the death of Mrs. Wyatt, testified that she was very drunk and in a belligerent mood. If you're looking for sour notes, you have one right there: belligerent drunks pick fights with other people, not themselves. But this is pretty slim—belligerence can turn to depression at the drop of another martini, or, as in this case, *tequila.* In any case, the police here—and they're not as carefree and inefficient as you've probably been led to believe—are thoroughly satisfied that Mrs. Wyatt's death was a suicide. They released her body and her effects to her sister in San Diego, Mrs. Earl Sullivan.

As I said at the beginning of this report, everything at this end *seems* on the up and up. There is a puzzling factor involved which may have something to do with the case, and then again it may not. I give it to you for what it's worth.

It concerns Joe O'Donnell, the man you asked me to investigate. He dropped out of sight a week ago. He's been hanging around the Windsor bar every night for over a year. When he didn't show up three or four nights in a row Emilio, the head bartender, paid a visit to his apartment. O'Donnell wasn't there and hadn't been seen by any of the neighbors for some time. His landlady claimed he skipped out because he owed back rent. This may be true but it doesn't explain his absence from the bar, which he used to call his "office." Emilio was vague on what kind of business O'Donnell conducted from his "office," but he insisted it was legitimate, that O'Donnell had never been in trouble with the police or the management of the hotel. My guess is that he went in for any petty con game that came along, whether it was accepting loans from wealthy women he picked up, like Mrs. Wyatt; organizing poker parties for American businessmen, taking bets on the horses, stuff like that. Nothing illegal, nothing big-time. O'Donnell has—or had—a lot of charm, apparently. Everyone has a good word to say for him: generous, kind, amusing, intelligent, good-looking. How come this superman is cadging drinks and playing gigolo at a bar every night? It doesn't add up.

I questioned Emilio further. It seemed odd to me that a bartender should go checking up on a customer simply because he failed to appear for a few nights. Emilio was evasive—Mexicans are, usually, but they lie to please rather than to deceive, and once you understand this, it's easy to cope with. It turned out that a letter had been delivered to the hotel in care of Emilio, addressed to Joe O'Donnell. It had been sent airmail from San Francisco, and on the envelope the sender had written "*urgente y importante.*"

When Emilio handed the letter over to O'Donnell, O'Donnell made some remark about being an Easterner and not even knowing anyone in San Francisco except people he'd met casually in the Windsor bar. Like Mrs. Kellogg and Mrs. Wyatt, I presume. Anyway, he sat down and read the letter over a bottle of beer. Emilio asked him, half kidding, what was so "*urgente y importante,*" and O'Donnell told him to mind his own goddamn business. He got up and left the bar immediately and that's the last anyone's seen of him.

Naturally, Emilio's curiosity was aroused. Ever since Mrs. Wyatt's death, he's had suicide on his mind. For reasons not entirely religious, suicide has a more profound effect on the average Mexican than any other kind of violence. Emilio went to O'Donnell's apartment in the vague fear that O'Donnell had killed himself because of some very bad news he'd received in the letter.

Well, there you have it. I know O'Donnell's address and will check on him further. Also I've arranged with Emilio to contact me when and if O'Donnell shows up at the bar. He might. Then again he might be in Africa by this time. He would have no trouble getting out of the country since he's an American citizen and not in any trouble with the authorities.

To get back to Mr. and Mrs. Kellogg. They checked out of the Windsor early on the morning of September thirteenth and took a cab to the airport. There was no sign of the nurse Kellogg had told the hospital authorities he intended to hire to accompany his wife on the trip. Maybe he changed his mind, maybe he arranged to meet the nurse at the airport.

When they left the hotel, Mrs. Kellogg was wearing a bandage over her left temple and she had a black eye. According to the doorman, she acted as though she'd been drugged, but I'd be inclined to take this with a grain of salt. It may be a case of that national characteristic of lying to please—i.e., he assumed from my questions that I suspected something was wrong and he was merely trying to "help."

I await further instructions. Best,

FOWLER.

Dodd read the report through a second time, then he buzzed for Lorraine.

"Send a wire to Fowler."

"Straight or night letter?"

"Night letter."

"O.K., you have fifty words." She copied Fowler's address from the envelope containing the report. "Shoot."

"Check all means of exit for O'Donnell. Search apartment for letters, bank statements, photographs, evidence of love interests. Get names of all friends he might contact. Keep up the good work. Sincerely. Dodd."

"That's not fifty words," Lorraine said.

"So?"

"Maybe you should add something, like 'give my best to your wife.'"

"I could," Dodd said, "but it might not be in the best of taste. He's a widower."

"Oh. But if you're paying for fifty words, and it's almost two dollars…"

"Kindly send it as is, with no further editing. After that I'd like you to call Moffett Field and get the address and phone number of a pilot named Bert Reiner. I don't know his rank. He lives in Mountain View with his wife."

Lorraine rose. "Well, that's a change from kennels and dog hospitals anyway."

"You'll get back to them."

"If I only knew *why* you wanted to find this Scottie, it would make my work less boring. I mean, I'm your secretary, I should *know* these things."

"Maybe you should, at that. Remind me to tell you, for Christmas."

The exchange had given Lorraine a headache. She took an aspirin to relieve the pain, half a tranquilizer to quiet her nerves, and a vitamin pill on general principles. Then she reached for the telephone again.

13

The town of Mountain View cowered under the benevolent despotism of the jet age. Its older residents held public meetings and wrote letters of protest to the newspapers, complaining of sonic booms and broken windows, flaming crashes and altered skies. In return, the air-force personnel and some of the more war-conscious citizens wrote letters which said in effect, "Where would you be without jet protection in case of attack?"

The Reiners lived in the lower half of a new redwood duplex near El Camino Real. Betty Reiner answered the door. She was a tall, slim, pretty brunette with green eyes and an automatic smile that looked less genial than a frown. She wore tight black Capri pants, a silk shirt, and a double strand of pearls that reached below her hips. Dodd wondered whether this was her ordinary housekeeping costume or if she had dressed for the occasion.

"I don't know what this is all about," she told Dodd as she led him into an immaculate black and white living room. "I was just going to have some coffee. Would you like some?"

"Thanks, I would."

"Sugar and cream?"

"A little of both."

She poured the coffee out of a white ceramic pot with a black lacquered handle. The only touches of color in the room were Mrs. Reiner's green eyes and the orange polish on her fingernails. "I wish I had a nickel for every cup of coffee I've doled out on the job. As soon as the passengers realized it was free they couldn't get enough of the stuff." She handed him his coffee. "So Smitty sent you here, eh?"

"Yes. He thought you might have some information I need."

"What gave him that idea?"

"He told me you had practically a photographic memory."

Mrs. Reiner was too shrewd to be taken in by such obvious flattery. "It's not that good. Some things I remember, some I don't. What do you have in mind?"

"A certain flight from Mexico City to San Francisco."

"Which one? I've made that trip fifty times."

"Saturday, September thirteen."

"That was about a week before I was fired. I suppose Smitty told you? They fired me when they found out I was married. It's a crazy rule. If marriage interferes with efficiency, why doesn't the Air Force discharge my husband and all the other married pilots. You'd think being a stewardess was some fancy, high-toned job when all you do really is play waitress and maid, without tips."

"Saturday, September thirteen," Dodd repeated patiently. "The pilot and co-pilot were Robert Forbes and James Billings, and the two stewardesses working with you were Ann Mackay and Maria Fernandez. Do you recall now?"

"Of course. That was the week end a friend of mine got sick and I offered to return to Mexico City that night and take her place on the same flight the next day. It was against the rules, but as I said, they've got some crazy rules."

Dodd opened the manila folder marked A. KELLOGG and took out the pictures of Amy. "This woman, I have reason to believe, boarded your plane with her husband and possibly a third party."

Mrs. Reiner studied the pictures with interest but no immediate recognition. "She looks like a hundred other people I've seen. Was there anything special about her?"

"Two things. She wore a bandage over her left temple and she had a black eye."

"The woman with the black eye—of course I remember! Maria and I were kidding around about it, wondering how she got it, whether her husband beat her up or something. He didn't seem like the type. A good-looking man, very quiet and considerate."

"Considerate of whom?"

"Well, of her, mainly. But of us girls too. A lot of passengers get pretty demanding in the course of a long flight. He didn't ask for anything special. Neither did she. She slept most of the time."

"Quite a few stewardesses are also registered nurses. Are you, Mrs. Reiner?"

"No."

"Had any nursing experience at all?"

"Just the elementary stuff included in our training course, how to cope with air sickness, how to administer oxygen to asthmatics and cardiac patients, things like that."

"Then you wouldn't know if Mrs. Kellogg's sleep was a natural one or not."

"What do you mean 'natural'?"

"Is there any possibility that she was drugged?"

Mrs. Reiner fidgeted with her rope of pearls. "Her husband gave her some Dramamine."

"How do you know it was Dramamine?"

"Well, it was a little white pill that looked just like it."

"A lot of narcotics and barbiturates are in the form of little white pills."

"I guess I just assumed it was Dramamine because so many passengers use it these days. Don't forget, Dramamine makes some people very sleepy. Maybe the effect's only psychological, but it happens." She tied the pearls in a knot, untied them, reached for her coffee. "I can't believe—I don't want to believe—that one of my passengers was being doped against her will, right under my nose."

"Did she make any fuss about taking the pill, or pills?"

"I only saw her take one. There may have been others. She didn't make a fuss, no, but I thought she looked a little scared. Not about taking the pill, just scared in general. A lot of my passengers do look scared, though, especially when the weather's bad."

"Were Mr. and Mrs. Kellogg traveling alone or was there a third party with them?"

"They were alone."

"Are you sure? Mr. Kellogg was supposed to have hired a nurse to accompany his wife on the trip."

"They were alone," Mrs. Reiner repeated firmly. "They paid no attention to anyone else, as far as I know. Lots of times when we're passing over something interesting, the passengers will get out of their seats and fraternize. Mr. and Mrs. Kellogg didn't."

"This was a first-class flight?"

"Yes."

"Double row of seats on each side of the aisle?"

"Yes. Mrs. Kellogg was in the window seat."

"Who was sitting across the aisle from Mr. Kellogg?"

Mrs. Reiner wrinkled her forehead, then smoothed out the wrinkles with the tips of her fingers. "I can't swear to it but I think it was a couple of Mexican women, looked like mother and daughter."

"Which one had the aisle seat?"

"I don't remember. You don't seem to understand, Mr. Dodd. When you've made that same flight dozens of times as I did, it's hard to differentiate them. Why, I would never even have recognized Mrs. Kellogg's picture if you hadn't clued me in about the black eye. It takes something special like that to make one trip stand out in my memory."

"Now that this particular flight is standing out, you're remembering more and more about it?"

"Yes. There was a little girl up front who kept getting sick. And an elderly man, a cardiac patient. I had to give him oxygen."

Dodd said, "I understand the airline keeps a list of the passengers on board each flight."

"There are several such lists. I had my own."

"What other information was on this passenger list?"

"Where each of them was going."

"Where were the Kelloggs going?"

"They had return tickets to San Francisco. We only made one other stop, Los Angeles." She reached for the coffeepot again, but her hand suddenly stopped in midair. "Now that's funny. I could have sworn that the Kelloggs were booked through to San Francisco, and yet... Wait a minute. Let me reconstruct. The plane landed at L.A. and everybody got off, as usual, for the stopover, except the cardiac patient. I stayed behind with him. He was scared, poor guy, so I gave him all the attention I could. We were in flight again before I had a chance to resume my regular duties, making the new passengers comfortable, handing out pillows and so on. I went to the rear of the plane... I remember now," she went on, her voice rising a little with excitement. "As I passed by, I saw that there were two women in the seats where the Kelloggs had been sitting. I was just about to tell the women that those seats were taken when I noticed that Mrs. Kellogg's coat and carryall bag and Mr. Kellogg's hat and brief case were missing from the baggage rack."

"They got off at L.A., then?"

"Yes. I might have been mistaken, though, about their tickets being through to San Francisco."

"You weren't."

"It seems peculiar, doesn't it? But then, I'm sure there's some logical explanation."

"I'm sure there's an explanation," Dodd said. "I'm just not sure how logical it is. In case you remember anything else, no matter how trivial it may be, call me at one of these numbers, any time."

"All right."

"And thank you very much, Mrs. Reiner, for the information."

"I hope you can use it."

"I can use it."

After he'd gone she sat down and poured herself the rest of the pot of coffee. Now that the flight had been singled out clearly in her mind, she couldn't stop thinking about it. By the time the plane landed at San Francisco, the old man with the heart condition was in bad shape and had to be taken off the field in an ambulance. The little girl who'd been airsick recovered in time to chew several wads of gum and get some of it stuck in her hair. It was removed with patience and an ice cube. The honeymoon couple departed with their transistor radio tuned into the final inning of a baseball game. The smart alec with the flask and the bum jokes almost fell off the landing platform. The two Mexican women who'd been sitting across the aisle from the Kelloggs and looked like mother and daughter, couldn't have been; they left the plane separately and without speaking. The younger one had her purse clutched in both hands as if it contained her whole future.

"It was just an ordinary routine flight," she said aloud, as if Dodd had been there to deny it. "Nothing sinister about it. Mrs. Kellogg's black eye was the result of an accident, not a beating up. The pill her husband gave her was Dramamine. She looked scared because she didn't like traveling by plane. They got off at Los Angeles because—well, there could have been any number of reasons: Mrs. Kellogg's condition, or Mr. Kellogg's suddenly remembering a business deal, or both of them deciding to visit a relative they hadn't seen for a long time."

A group of jets roared overhead in take-off. The house shook, the windows rattled, the sky changed.

14

Helene Brandon planned the trip to the city as a surprise for Gill. Shortly before noon she appeared at his office looking chic and cheerful in her sable-trimmed suit and best pearls.

Gill's private secretary, Mrs. Keely, greeted her with restraint: *A wife's place is in her own office, not her husband's.* "Good morning, Mrs. Brandon. Mr. Brandon is not expecting you?"

"No, he's not. This is a surprise."

"Oh. He's very busy this morning. He left orders that he was not to be disturbed until lunch time."

"It's lunch time now."

She opened the door of his office, softly, in case he was dictating or talking on the telephone. But he was doing neither. He was bent over his desk, his head buried in his hands, while the ticker-tape machine beside him coughed politely for attention. She stood, quiet and motionless, watching him, thinking with surprise how vulnerable he looked and wishing she had never seen him like this. She would rather have had him arguing with her, shouting at her, criticizing her, anything but sitting there defenseless.

"Gill?"

He raised his head slowly. His eyes were red, as though he'd been rubbing them, trying to erase from them images he didn't want to see. "Hello, Helene."

"Your secretary told me you were busy. Are you?"

"Yes."

"Doing what?"

"Thinking."

"Not about… Oh Gill, stop it, stop worrying over things you can't do anything about."

"I have more reason to worry now than at any time since she disappeared."

"Why? Has something happened?" She crossed the room and put her hands on his shoulders. They seemed frail and stooped under the padded cashmere coat. "Gilly, dear. Tell me."

"Amy never came home that night, Sunday. Rupert came home alone. Every word he's spoken is a rotten lie."

"I can't believe… How do you *know?*"

"Dodd found out."

"Can you trust him?"

"Further than I can Rupert."

His shoulders twitched impatiently under her embrace. She stepped back, and her hands dropped to her sides. Thoughts began swimming to the surface of her mind, ugly and sharp-toothed, like barracuda coming out of the ambush of kelp and crevice. *I don't care if she never came home, never comes home, never is seen again.*

"They left Mexico City together on Saturday," Gill said, "bound for San Francisco. Their luggage was checked through. It arrived, but they didn't. They got off at Los Angeles. Their luggage wasn't claimed until Sunday evening."

"What does that prove?"

"It proves what I've suspected all along, that Rupert's whole story is a pack of lies. Amy didn't come home Sunday night, she didn't pick up her dog, he didn't drive her to any station, the highball glass with the lipstick stains wasn't hers…"

"How can you be sure of all that? Maybe they got off at Los Angeles together and took a plane up here the next day, still together."

"Why would they stop over in Los Angeles without any luggage? A man traveling alone might. No woman would." He stopped to rub his eyes again. "There is some evidence that Rupert doped her to make her more—manageable."

"Doped her? Why, that's crazy, that's utterly crazy!"

"I think," he said quietly, "you'd prefer to believe that I'm crazy rather than that Rupert is corrupt. Is that right, Helene?"

She leaned, suddenly and heavily, against the desk. "I—I've never said you were crazy, just some of your ideas."

"You're convinced, aren't you, that I have some sort of fixation on Amy which puts me in a position where I can't evaluate facts. Go on, admit it, Helene. You've been thinking it for a long time, tossing hints, making implications. You might as well say it outright."

Her mouth moved carefully, like a cornered animal feeling its way out of a trap. "I don't believe either that you're crazy or that Rupert is corrupt."

"You're straddling the fence, eh?"

"I'm trying to be detached and reasonable."

"You're detached, all right. I think you've been detached for a long time, from Amy, from me too."

She could feel words boiling in her throat like lye, but she swallowed them all and said calmly, "I couldn't be detached from you, Gill, you know that. But that doesn't mean I must agree with you on everything, all the time. You don't like Rupert and never have. I do."

"Why? Because he married Amy and took her off our hands?"

It was close to the truth. "I thought he would make a good husband for her. And he has, until..."

"Until. Yes. That's a very large word."

"Oh, Gill, stop it. Don't put me in the position of having to defend Rupert against you."

"You're defending him against the facts, not me. The *facts*. Do you hear me?"

"I'm sure everyone in the building can hear you."

"Let them!"

They glared at each other across the desk. But deeper than Helene's anger was a feeling of relief. *He's shouting, that's good. At least he doesn't look so vulnerable any more. He's fighting, not just sitting with his neck bent and exposed as if to a guillotine.*

"While we're airing grievances," he said, more softly, "I must ask you not to wear your pearls when you take the train up to the city."

"Why not?"

"There've been too many jewel robberies lately."

"The pearls are insured."

"Not for what they're worth. And I can't afford to replace them. You might as well find out now, money's tight. Call it bad luck on my part, or poor judgment, or both. But the fact is, we have to cut down, perhaps even sell the house."

"Sell our house?"

"It might come to that."

"Why didn't you tell me before? There are a hundred ways I could have been saving money."

"You can start now."

"I don't mind." But it was more than not minding; she felt quite excited at the idea of a change, a challenge. Perhaps they could find a ramshackle old house, and Gill and the kids could all help fixing it up, painting, putting on a new roof, making over curtains, repairing doors and steps. The whole family working together for a common purpose...

"I've been poor before. I don't mind."

"I do," Gill said. "I mind very much."

She could still see the old house clearly in her mind, but no one was working on it. The roof leaked, the steps sagged, the windows were cracked and curtainless, the paint was peeling, and Gill was sitting on the front porch, his head in his hands, his neck exposed to any blow, any attack. "God damn you," she said. "Stand up and fight."

"Fight? Fight what? You?"

"Not me. You shouldn't be fighting me. We should be on the same side, pulling together. And we would be if…"

"If what? Let me hear your 'ifs', Helene."

"If it weren't for Amy."

He looked pained but not surprised. "You may regret saying that."

"Maybe I already do," she said soberly. "But not because I don't believe it."

The intercom signaled for attention, and the voice of Gill's secretary insinuated itself into the room, as penetrating and genteel as the whisper of a lady librarian. "Mr. Dodd is on the telephone again, Mr. Brandon. Will you take the call?"

"Go ahead… Dodd? Yes. Yes, I understand. When? How much? Good God, didn't anyone try to stop him? I know it's legal, but under the circumstances… No, I can't get away from the office until later this afternoon. Hold on a minute." Gill put his hand over the telephone and spoke sharply to his wife, "I must ask you to wait outside."

"Why?"

"This is a personal matter."

"Meaning it's about Amy?"

"Meaning it's none of your business."

"I couldn't care less," she said airily, but her cheeks burned red and when she walked to the door her legs felt weak and rubbery.

She stopped at the secretary's desk in the outer office. "Tell Mr. Brandon I couldn't wait. I have another—appointment."

Appointment wasn't quite the word, she thought, as she rode the elevator downstairs. Errand was closer. Errand of mercy. Or perhaps errand of mischief. It would depend on your viewpoint.

On the street she hailed a cab and gave the driver the address of Rupert's office.

"That's walking distance," he said.

"I know. I'm in a hurry."

"O.K. You from the Peninsula?"

"Yes."

He screwed up his face in soundless laughter. "I can always tell. After twenty-six years in this business you get intuition. I'm from the Peninsula myself. Redwood City. Every morning I take the train up here and I drive my cab all day and then I take the train back. Always been crazy about trains. The wife says I ought to of been an engineer. That way I wouldn't always be running into a bunch of knucklehead cops always telling me where to park and what to do and making with the one-way streets. You waste a lot of gas on these one-way streets."

You waste a lot of gas, period, Helene thought irritably. Any other time the cabbie would have amused her, she would have asked questions, drawn him out, and later made a funny story of the incident to tell Gill and the kids. Today he seemed merely a talkative, annoying old man with a grievance.

He parked at a red curb. She paid him and got out of the cab as quickly as possible.

When she reached Rupert's office, she found Miss Burton in the act of combing her hair.

"Why, Mrs. Brandon," Miss Burton said, returning the comb to her purse with nervous haste. "We weren't expecting you."

Editorial "we" or Rupert-and-I "we," Helene wondered. She had never paid particular attention to Miss Burton in the past, and she wouldn't have now if it weren't for Gill's suspicions. There was nothing special about her: eyes blue and rather solemn, short turned-up nose, plump, pink cheeks, temporary blond hair, short, sturdy legs intended for long and loyal service. The composite picture she presented was one of directness and simplicity; not even Gill, with his emotional astigmatism, could have denied that.

Helene said casually, "Is Mr. Kellogg around?"

"He just left."

"I'll wait, if I may. Or perhaps I'll do some shopping and come back later."

"He won't be in the office any more today," Miss Burton said. "He's not feeling well. I think he's coming down with the flu. He hasn't been taking good care of himself since Mrs. Kel—since he's been living alone."

"Oh."

"I mean, well, no proper meals for one thing. Good hot meals are very important."

"Do you cook, Miss Burton?"

"Cook?" She flushed from the base of her throat to the tips of her ears. "Why? Why do you ask that?"

"I'm just interested."

"I like to cook when there's someone to cook for. Only there isn't. I think that answers your question, and the other questions behind it."

"Other questions?"

"I think you know what I mean."

"But I don't. I have no idea."

"Your husband has." Miss Burton's voice trembled, and a pulse

138

began to beat, hard and unrhythmically, in her left temple. "Lots of ideas."

"Has he been talking to you?"

"To me? No. Not *to* me. Behind my back. Hiring a greasy little detective to follow me, pump me—well, he was pumping at a dry well. He didn't find out a thing, the same as you're not going to because there's nothing to find out, because I never…"

"Wait a minute. Do you think I came here at my husband's request?"

"It's a funny coincidence, last night the detective, now you."

Helene's brief laugh was more like a cough of indignation. "Why, if Gill knew I was here, he'd—well, no matter. Let's put it this way. I don't agree with my husband on everything. If you're angry with him for something he's done, all right, that's your privilege. But don't let your anger spill over on me. I came here as a friend of Rupert's. You're his friend, too… Aren't you?"

"Yes."

"Well, then, hadn't we better work together, cooperate?"

Miss Burton shook her head, more in sorrow than in denial. "I don't know. I don't know who I can trust any more."

"That puts two of us in the same boat. The question is, where's the boat going? And who's at the helm?"

"I don't know anything about boats." Miss Burton's voice was cold and cautious. "Not a thing."

"Neither do I, really. I went sailing once on the Bay with my husband. Years ago, just the two of us. Gill was the skipper and I was supposed to be the crew. God, it was awful. I was scared to begin with, because I can't swim very well, and then a strong wind came up and Gill began shouting orders at me. Only I couldn't understand them, they sounded like a foreign language or a child's gibberish—ready about, hard alee, jibe ho. Gill explained them all to me afterwards, but at the time I felt such terrible confusion, as if some immediate and urgent action was expected of me but I couldn't understand what. That's the way I feel now, right this minute. There's a strong wind, there's danger, I should be doing something. But I don't know what. The orders sound like gibberish, I can't even tell where they're coming from. And I can't get off the boat. Can you?"

"I haven't tried."

"And you won't try?"

"No. It's too late."

"Then we'd better get our signals straight," Helene said bluntly. "Don't you agree?"

"I guess so."

"Where's Rupert?"

"I told you, he wasn't feeling well, he went home."

"Straight home?"

"He may have stopped for lunch. He always eats at the same place at noon, Lassiter's, on Market Street, near Kearny."

Lassiter's was a moderately priced bar and grill that catered to the men of the financial district. They were a martini crowd, consisting of third vice-presidents, sales managers, West Coast representatives, all of them known as executives, a word which meant nothing except that it entitled them to a two-hour lunch.

She spotted Rupert immediately, sitting at the counter with a bottle of beer and a hamburger in front of him, both untouched. An open paperback book was propped against the beer bottle, and he was staring at it but not reading it. He looked tense and expectant, as if he was waiting for someone he didn't like or something he didn't want to face.

When she touched him lightly on the shoulder he jumped and the book fell on its side and the beer bottle teetered.

She said, "Aren't you going to eat your lunch?"

"No."

"I hate to see anything wasted."

"Help yourself."

He got up and she took his place at the counter and reached for the hamburger without embarrassment or self-consciousness.

He stood behind her while she ate. "What are you doing here, Helene?"

"Miss Burton told me you usually had lunch at this place so I came over and here you are."

"And now what?"

She spoke quickly and quietly so the man on the next stool wouldn't overhear. "Gill just had a phone call. From Dodd. I'm sure it was about you and some money. I could only hear Gill's part of the conversation and not much of that. He asked me to wait outside so I couldn't hear any more, but I think he's going to meet Dodd late this afternoon. They may be planning some kind of showdown."

"About the money?"

"I guess so."

"They have no grounds."

The man on the next stool paid his check and left, and Rupert sat down in his place.

"Listen," Helene said. "I've got to know more about this. I've put myself in a bad position trying to defend you. I want to be reassured that I'm doing the right thing."

"You are."

"What money was Dodd talking about?"

"I cashed a check on Amy's account, using her power of attorney."

"Why?"

"Why do people cash checks? Because they need money."

"No, I meant why all the fuss on Dodd's part, and Gill's? Gill said it was legal but that someone should have stopped you, under the circumstances."

"No one could have stopped me. No one even has the right to question me about it. As a matter of fact, whatever employee of the bank informed Dodd about the check was guilty of improper conduct. Dodd holds no official position, and private records shouldn't be open to him."

"What's he like?"

"I don't know. I've never met him."

"Miss Burton has," she said, with deliberation. "Last night."

He tried to look indifferent. She could see his face in the mirror behind the counter, trying on various expressions none of which seemed to fit. He said finally, "So she couldn't keep her mouth shut."

"She didn't intend to tell me anything, don't be hard on her. She thought I'd come to the office as a spy for the great Brandon-Dodd combine. That's a laugh, isn't it?" She pushed away the empty plate with an expression of distaste as if she'd suddenly decided that she hadn't been hungry after all and now regretted eating the hamburger. "Miss Burton's in love with you, I suppose you know that."

"No, I don't!" he said sharply. "You're imagining…"

"It's time you found out, then. It's written all over her, Rupert. I feel rather bad about it."

"Why should you?"

"Oh, empathy, I guess. It's happened to me too, being in love with someone who hardly noticed me. That was years ago, of course," she added quickly. "Before I met Gill."

"Of course."

"Are you in a hurry?"

"Why?"

"You keep looking at that clock on the wall."

"Well, I have to get back to the office pretty soon."

"I thought you weren't going back to the office this afternoon."

"What gave you that idea?"

"Miss Burton."

"Miss Burton," he said easily, "almost managed to convince me I wasn't feeling well and should go home. The fact is, I'm fine and I intend to spend the afternoon working." He swung round on the stool as if he intended to get up and leave. Instead, after a second's hesitation, he completed the full circle and faced the counter again. "Let's have some coffee, eh?"

The maneuver would have been obvious even if she hadn't already been suspicious of him. By tilting her head slightly, Helene could see in the mirror the reflection of the entrance door. A young woman had just come in and was surveying the room with an air of anxiety. She was well built and pretty, dressed in a skin-tight woolen suit, a feathered hat, half a dozen strings of colored glass beads, and patent leather pumps with heels so high that she stood at a forward angle as if she were bucking a high wind. When she put up her hand to adjust the feathered hat over her blond curls, a platinum wedding band gleamed under the lights.

"She's rather pretty," Helene said.

"Who is?"

"The young woman by the door. She appears to be looking for someone."

"I hadn't noticed."

"Well, notice now."

"Why should I?"

"Oh, you might be interested. She is. She's coming your way."

143

"She can't be. I've never seen her before in my life."

Rupert turned and gave the girl a long, cold, deliberate stare. She stopped abruptly, then headed for the cigarette machine, moving with little wobbly steps on the high, narrow heels. Helene noticed that her feet were proportionately larger than the rest of her, very wide and flat, as if she'd spent a considerable period of her life walking barefoot. When she had fished the cigarettes out of the trough, the girl put them in her black patent leather handbag and walked toward the exit. One of the men sitting at a table gave a low whistle as she passed, but she paid no attention, as if she hadn't heard the sound or didn't know what it meant or for whom it was intended.

"I think she's a farm girl," Helene said. "That getup looks like something she's copied from a movie magazine. I suppose you might call her a blonde with a good tan or a brunette with a good bleach job, depending on your viewpoint."

"I have no viewpoint. I don't know the woman."

"She's probably one of the secretaries in your office building and has a mad, mad crush on you."

"You're being ridiculous. I'm not the type of man women get crushes on."

"Oh, but you are. You make a perfectly splendid father image, firm but kindly, strong but gentle, that sort of thing. It's fatal—for a girl that age. How old would you say she is? Twenty-two? Twenty-five?"

"I haven't thought about it and don't intend to."

"Years and years younger than Miss Burton, anyway, wouldn't you say?"

"Stop playing games."

Helene smiled. "I like games. If I didn't, I wouldn't be here. It's kind of amusing, isn't it, Gill and Dodd sniffing around like

144

a pair of nervous bloodhounds and me trying to put them off the scent? Your scent."

"Why are you trying?"

"I told you, I like games."

"I like games too, when the grand prize isn't my own skin. This is the second time you've warned me about Gill's activities. What's your real reason, Helene?"

"It's too complicated to explain."

"Don't explain, then," he said.

"I won't."

"I want to thank you, anyway, for all the trouble you've gone to."

"You're welcome. At least I think you're welcome. I don't know. I—I'm beginning to feel like a traitor. I'd like to be reassured that I'm not, that I've done the right thing in coming here."

"You've done the right thing," he said gravely. "Thank you again, Helene. Someday, perhaps soon, Amy will be here to thank you too."

"Amy? Soon?"

"I hope so."

"She's coming back?"

"Of course she's coming back. What made you think she wasn't?"

"Nothing—special."

"Maybe by Thanksgiving, or at least by Christmas, we'll all be together again. Everything will be the same as it always was."

"The same," she repeated dully. "Of course. Precisely the same."

Precisely. Inevitably. Irrevocably.

She rose, one hand pressed against her mouth to stifle a sound she could never let anyone else hear.

Later, when she was asked, she couldn't remember exactly how she spent the next couple of hours. She recalled walking along many streets, staring into the windows of shops and the faces of strangers. For a long, or a little, time she sat on a bench in Union Square watching sad-eyed old men feed bread crumbs and popcorn to the pigeons. The pigeons were plump and sleek and did not resemble Amy at all, but Helene drew back in protest when one of them came too close to her foot. She was repelled by its dependence, its insistent docility, which it seemed to be forcing on her. *Amy. Amy again. By Thanksgiving. Or Christmas. No hope of never.*

It started to rain lightly and the old men abandoned their benches and ambled off to shelter. Helene put on her gloves and rose, ready to leave, when she saw the girl from Lassiter's grill entering the Square from Powell Street. She had no idea whether the girl would recognize her or whether it would be important if she did, but simply as a precaution she picked up a discarded newspaper from the grass and held it in front of her as a spying shield.

She thought at first that the girl was alone and that the man walking parallel to her was just about to pass her and be on his own way. He didn't pass. He kept right on walking beside her but at a distance, as if the two of them were in the midst or the aftermath of a quarrel. They approached the bench where Helene sat hidden behind the limp newspaper, with the pigeons cooing and coaxing at her feet.

The man had the same startling color contrast as the girl, very light hair and deeply tanned skin. They might have been brother and sister. The man was the older of the two, perhaps in his early thirties. There were clearly defined laugh lines around his eyes and mouth, but he wasn't laughing. He looked pale under his tan, and feeble under the loud plaid sport coat. Helene had never seen him before but she remembered others like him. Years ago during the depression in Oakland, her way to school led her past a poolroom where jobless young men used to hang out for lack of anything better to do. On their faces, in their posture, they all shared a common expression, not bitter or angry, but listless, as if they hadn't expected much anyway. The man in the plaid coat wore the same expression.

The farm girl and the poolroom buff. They looked out of place in the Square and with each other. She couldn't imagine what connection either of them could have with Rupert. I must have been mistaken, she thought. Rupert was telling me the truth when he said he didn't know the girl, had never seen her before. He's probably been telling the truth about everything. Suspicion is contagious. I caught it from Gill.

It was nearly four o'clock when she returned to Gill's office and found him with his topcoat on and his briefcase under his arm, ready to depart.

"You're soaking wet," he said. "Where have you been?"

"Oh, walking. Looking at things."

"If you hurry, you can catch the 4:37 train home."

"Aren't you coming too?"

"Later. I have to see Dodd."

"Why?"

"It's time we had a showdown with Rupert."

"But why now, today?"

"The dog's been found."

She looked at him stupidly. "Dog? What…"

"Amy's dog," he said.

15

"The Sidalia Kennels," Dodd said. "It's a combination small-animal hospital and boarding kennel on Skyline Boulevard just outside the city limits. He brought the dog in Sunday night, the fourteenth of September. The vet himself wasn't there but a college kid, a Cal Aggie student who helps out during the summer, was on duty at the time. The dog had a spot of eczema on his back and Kellogg's instructions were to keep him there until further notice. He paid a month's board in advance. The dog was wearing a plaid harness but no leash. He's in good shape, according to the vet; the eczema's gone and he's ready to leave whenever Kellogg wants to pick him up... Did you call Kellogg's office, by the way?"

Gill nodded. "Miss Burton said he left at noon to go home."

"We'll catch him there then. You understand, don't you, that there's nothing much we can do except ask him questions and hope for answers. It's not illegal to park a dog at a kennel. And it's not illegal to use a power of attorney, even fifteen thousand dollars' worth."

"What would he want with all that money?"

"Let's go and find out. We'll take my car if you don't mind."

With the slackening of the rain, a wind had risen, and the little Volkswagen wavered with the gusts as if it were going to roll like tumbleweed across the road. But there was no place for it to roll. All the way out Fulton Street the five o'clock traffic moved bumper to bumper. Gill sat with his fists clenched against his thighs, and every time Dodd applied the brakes, Gill's foot stamped on the floorboard.

"It's a little car," Dodd said after a time. "It only needs one driver."

"Sorry."

"There's no need to get all tensed up about this, Brandon. When we confront him with what we know of the truth, he may break down and tell us the rest of it. Then again, he may have a nice pat explanation for everything."

"Including the money?"

"The money part's easy. He needed it to send to Amy—her expenses in New York are running higher than she expected."

"She isn't in New York."

"So if I were Kellogg, I'd say, prove it."

"I will, even if I have to wring the truth out of him with my bare hands."

Dodd was silent a moment, apparently engrossed in guiding the car through the traffic which had thinned out somewhat west of Presidio Boulevard. "Come on now, Brandon. You're not really figuring on that bare-hand bit."

"I am."

"Why are you carrying a gun, then?"

"I—don't know. I bought it this afternoon. I've never owned a gun before. It suddenly occurred to me that I ought to have one, that I needed one."

"And now you feel better?"

"No."

"Nor do I," Dodd said grimly. "Get rid of it."

"That won't be necessary."

"I think it will. You're not the type who should be messing around with loaded guns."

"I guess I knew that," Gill said. "It's not loaded. I didn't buy any cartridges."

Dodd made a little sound that seemed to indicate amusement or relief or some of both. "I can't figure you, Brandon."

"If I wanted to be figured, as you put it, I would have gone to a psychiatrist, not a detective. Turn right at the next corner. The house is in the middle of the third block."

"You'd better leave the gun in the car."

"Why? It's not loaded."

"Kellogg might get the idea that it is, and counter with one of his own that *is* loaded. That would leave us out on a pretty thin limb."

"Have it your way." Gill handed over the gun and Dodd locked it inside the glove compartment.

"There's one more thing, Brandon. Let me do the talking. At first, anyway. You can horn in later if you like, but right at the beginning let's not get this thing slobbered up with emotions."

Gill got out of the car, stiffly. "I don't like your choice of language."

Dodd's reply was lost in the wind. He pulled up the collar of his coat and followed Gill up the walk to the porch.

It was a middle-income neighborhood where great attention was paid to outward appearances. Lawns no bigger than an elephant's ear were groomed to perfection, hedges barely had time to grow before they were clipped. The roses and camellias were fed almost as well and regularly as the occupants of the houses, and were probably given more care and inspection for signs of disease. It was a street of conformity; where identical houses were painted at the same time every spring, a place of rules where gardens, parenthood and the future were planned with equal care, and even if everything went wrong the master plan remained in effect—keep up appearances, clip the hedges, mow the lawn, so that no one will suspect that there's a third mortgage and that Mother's headaches are caused by martinis, not migraine.

Dodd asked, "Who picked the house?"

"Amy did." Gill pressed the door chime. "That is to say, she took my advice. The property was part of an estate sale which I found out about before it was announced on the open market."

"She could have afforded something more elaborate, though?"

"She could, yes. But not Rupert. Amy has always insisted on living within Rupert's income."

"Why?"

Gill looked annoyed, and Dodd wasn't sure whether it was the question that bothered him or the fact that no one was responding to the door chime.

"My sister," Gill said, "believes in the good old-fashioned type of marriage where the husband provides the financial support. It is not a case of stingi—of thriftiness."

The quick switch of words interested Dodd. *So he really thinks she's stingy. That probably means he's tried to borrow money from her and she refused. I wonder how hard up he actually is and to what degree his desperate need for Amy is more financial than brotherly.*

Inside the house a telephone began to ring. It rang eight times, ten times, then stopped for a few seconds and began again, as if the caller suspected that the first dialing had been incorrect.

"He's not here," Dodd said. "There's no use wasting our time."

"Wait just a few more minutes. He might be in the shower."

"Or in Santa Cruz."

"Why Santa Cruz?"

"No reason." Dodd shrugged. "I just picked the name out of a hat as a place to go when you don't want to stay where you are."

"You must have had a reason for picking that name rather than any other."

151

"It may not be valid."

"Let's hear it anyway."

It was getting dark. The lights in the houses on both sides of the street began coming on almost simultaneously. For a few moments, before drapes were drawn and blinds shut, the street had a festive air, a look of Christmas.

"It's just a hunch," Dodd said. "Suppose Kellogg decided to skip town, what would be the first thing he'd do?"

"Get some cash together."

"He already did that this morning. What do you think his next move might be?"

"I don't know."

"I don't know either; I'm just guessing. But judging from what I've heard about some of his characteristics, I have a notion he'd pick up his dog. The Sidalia Kennel is on Skyline Boulevard, and Skyline Boulevard leads to Santa Cruz. If he left the office at noon, as Miss Burton claims, he could easily be in Santa Cruz by this time. From there he'd probably head for L.A."

"Santa Cruz isn't on the direct route to L.A."

"He may be trying to avoid direct routes."

"We can't assume that he's left town," Gill said. "Why should he? He doesn't know we've found out about the dog and the cash."

"Someone may have tipped him off."

"That's impossible. No one else knows about it."

"No one?"

"Just my secretary. And my wife, Helene. You can rule them out, of course."

"Of course," Dodd said, but the ironic tone nullified the words. "Where is your wife now?"

"On her way home, on the train." Gill consulted his watch. "No, she'd be home by this time if she caught the 4:37. Why? Helene has nothing to do with this."

"I didn't say she had."

Inside the house the telephone began to ring again. Dodd turned toward the veranda steps. "Wait here a minute. I want to take a look around."

"I'll come with you."

"You'd better stay here. In case Kellogg or anyone else shows up you can sound a warning to me."

"Warning? What are you going to do?"

"On the police books—and I hope it doesn't get that far—it's called breaking and entering."

"You can't do that. It's illegal. I won't be a party to it. I've got too much to lose. My reputation…"

Dodd had already disappeared around the corner of the veranda where a steep driveway led into a double garage that was attached to the rear of the house. The overhead aluminum door was unlocked and rattling in the wind. Dodd pulled it open. Rupert's car, a two-year-old Buick, was parked inside, with the key in the ignition.

Dodd stood for a moment, with his hand on the hood of the car. The engine was cold. He took out his flashlight and aimed its beam at the door that led into the house. The lock was, as he'd hoped and expected, a flimsy one. The attached-garage setup often proved a boon to burglars: people who were careful about protecting their front door frequently put an inefficient lock on a door that opened into a garage. In a matter of minutes he had pried the lock loose with his pocketknife and the door was swinging inward.

He turned off the flashlight and stood in the near-darkness, listening for some sound that would indicate the house was occupied. But the wind was too noisy, and on top of the wind the telephone resumed its shrill demands for attention.

Dodd followed its sound across the room and picked up the receiver, hoping that the idea he had was wrong. "Hello?"

"Rupert? Is that you?"

It wasn't wrong. "Yes. I just got home... Helene?"

"I've been trying to reach you for an hour. Listen. Gill went to meet that detective. He's planning some kind of showdown with you because the dog's been found."

"Where?"

"I don't know where. All I know is you've been lying to me about the dog. Haven't you?... Well, *haven't* you?"

"Yes."

"And that girl in Lassiter's at noon, the one you said you'd never seen before, you knew her, didn't you? You'd arranged to meet her there, hadn't you?"

"Listen..."

"I won't listen any more. You've lied about everything. You've put me in an awful spot. I trusted you, I tried to help you. What if Gill finds out? He's crazy on the subject of Amy. He may do something terrible. I'm scared. I'm scared to death."

"Gill won't find out," Dodd said. "Take it easy."

"Everything's such a mess. I don't know what to do."

"Do nothing. I've got to go now, Helene. There's someone at the door."

"Gill?"

"Yes, I'm pretty sure it's Gill."

"Be careful of him," she said in a hurried whisper. "He's changed. I can't tell any more what he's thinking, what he's going to do."

"I'll be careful. You be discreet. Good-bye, Helene."

She began to cry. He hung up softly, wondering if she was the kind of woman who cried easily or if she was as scared of her husband as she claimed to be.

Dodd's eyes had become adjusted to the gloom. He could see the outlines of the furniture in the kitchen, the chrome-trimmed breakfast set, the yellow work counters, the matching stove and refrigerator. His gaze lingered on the refrigerator. The top part was intact, but at the bottom its outlines broke off suddenly as if the whole base of it had been blown out by dynamite. *No, that's crazy,* he thought. *There's no hole in the refrigerator, it's a shadow. Something has been put in front of it.*

His fingers moved carefully along the wall to the light switch and clicked it on. A man was lying face down on the floor in a widening pool of blood that reached almost to Dodd's feet. Beyond the man's outstretched left hand, which bore a gold wedding band, was a kitchen knife with a dark-stained, ten-inch blade. Someone had tried, without success, to clean up the mess. Two or three bloody bath towels were lying in the sink along with an overturned box of detergent.

Dodd thought first and irrationally of the little dog waiting at the kennel to be picked up by his master. It would be a long wait, a long, long wait.

He turned and fumbled his way down the dark hall to the front door. When he opened the door he saw Gill take a couple of steps backward as if he intended to run away.

"You'd better come inside for a minute," Dodd said.

"I don't like this, I don't like it at all. Is he—is he here?"

"He's here."

"How's he taking it, your breaking in like this?"

"He hasn't made any complaints."

"Oh. Well. In that case." Gill stepped inside, moving his body rigidly as if he expected an attack. "I can't see. Turn on the lights."

"Later. Where have you been all day, Brandon?"

"At my office. Why?"

"You didn't pay a call on your brother-in-law earlier in the afternoon?"

"Of course not."

"When you left the office to go out and buy that gun, was there anyone with you?"

"No."

"How long were you away?"

"What difference does it make?"

"Arranging for me to come here with you like this would make a good cover-up in the event that you were here earlier, by yourself."

"I don't know what the hell you're getting at. Why can't we turn on a light? Where's Rupert? What's going on?"

"Nothing's going on," Dodd said. "It's all over. Rupert's lying in the kitchen, dead."

"Dead? He—he killed himself?"

"Possibly but not probably. Someone tried to clean up the mess afterwards."

"Mess? How…?"

"A knife."

"Oh, God. Oh, my God. What am I going to do now?"

"You're going to come right back to the kitchen with me and phone the police."

"I won't. I can't. My family, my reputation. We've got to get out of here. Quick. Now. Before anyone comes. My God, fingerprints. Have I touched anything? The doorknob. I'll wipe off the doorknob…"

"Don't panic, Brandon." Dodd put his hand firmly on Gill's arm. "Take it easy."

"Let me go! I've got to get out of…"

"This is the wrong time to throw a fit, believe me. Now exercise some control, will you? I don't like this any better than you do. I could lose my license on this little gambit."

"It was your idea, it was all your idea."

"O.K., blame me if you like. Just don't flip your lid."

"What about Amy? Poor Amy, God help her."

"Amy isn't here. We are. If God's going to help anyone, I want priority. Now come on. We have work to do."

"I—I can't. I've never seen a—dead man before. I'm afraid I might be sick."

"Keep your head up and breathe through your mouth," Dodd said. "And kindly remember, as you view the remains, that you hated his guts anyway."

"You're a callous, insensitive brute."

"Sure. But right now you're stuck with me, so let's talk friendly."

As he spoke he gave Gill a little push and Gill started down the hall, holding a handkerchief to his mouth. When he reached the doorway of the kitchen he paused and let out a sound of surprise. The handkerchief fluttered to the floor, unnoticed.

"That's not," he said in a whisper, "that's not Rupert."

"Are you sure?"

"Rupert's bigger and his hair's much darker."

"Who is he, then?"

"I don't know. I can't see his face from here."

"Go over and take a look at it, then. Be careful not to touch him."

Gill walked cautiously around the pool of blood and leaned over the dead man. "I've never seen him before."

"Think hard, think of Rupert's friends, Amy's friends…"

"I don't know all of their friends, but I'm pretty sure this man wouldn't be one of them."

"What makes you say that?"

"That haircut, those clothes. He looks like a hoodlum or one of those beat boys that hang out around Grant Avenue."

"There's quite a difference between a hood and a bohemian."

"I'm simply saying that I don't believe Amy or Rupert would consort with a man like this."

"Then what's he doing in their kitchen?"

Gill's face was gray and shiny like wet putty. "For God's sake, how should I know? It's all crazy, preposterous."

"Well, you'd better call the police."

"Why me? Why can't you do it?"

"Because I won't be here when they arrive."

"You can't walk out and leave me holding the baby."

"I can. I have to."

"If you go, I go. I warn you, you're not getting out of here without me."

"Oh, for Christ's sake," Dodd said. "Take it easy and listen a minute, will you? We know now that Kellogg had a damn good reason to skip town. But his car's still in the garage. I want to find out how he left and if anyone was with him. I still think my hunch about the dog may be right, so I'm going to drive out to the kennel and check. If I stay here and wait for the police I'll lose several hours."

"But what will I tell them?"

"The truth. Why we came here together, how I got into the house, the exact truth. They'll probably send out either Ravick or Lipske of the Homicide squad. They're both friends of mine. They're not going to like my not sticking around, but tell them I'll contact them later and give them any information I have."

"Will I have to talk about—Amy?"

"You'll have to talk about everything. This is a murder case now."

Gill picked up his handkerchief from the floor and pressed it against his forehead. "I'd better call my lawyer."

"Yes, I think you'd better."

16

Along the ocean front waves angered by the wind were flinging themselves against the shore. Spray rose twenty feet in the air and swept across the highway like rain, leaving the surface sleek and treacherous. Dodd kept the speedometer at thirty, but the thundering of the sea and the great gusts of wind that shook and rattled the car gave him a sensation of speed and danger. The road, which he'd traveled a hundred times, seemed unfamiliar in the noisy darkness; it took turns he couldn't remember, past places he'd never seen. Just south of the zoo, the road curved inland to meet Skyline Boulevard.

The Sidalia Kennel was built on a bare, brown knoll about half a mile beyond the city limits. It looked new and clean, a brightly lit, two-story Colonial structure with an expanse of galvanized iron fencing on each side, and a small neon sign at the entrance to the driveway: PET HOSPITAL. A second sign below elaborated on the first: TREATMENT AND BOARDING. SMALL ANIMALS ONLY.

As Dodd got out of the car an Airedale began pacing up and down its runway in restless curiosity. A jet shrieked across the sky and the Airedale raised his head to howl a complaint.

"It's no use, old boy," Dodd said. "That's progress."

The howling had roused the other dogs. Before Dodd even reached the front door every runway had come alive with noise and movement: wagging tails, bared teeth, sounds of welcome and sounds of warning.

As Dodd reached out to press the buzzer the door opened to reveal a short, stout, white-haired man who looked a little like a beardless Santa Claus. He wore a smile and a white coat, both of them fresh and tidy.

"I'm Dr. Sidalia. Come in, come in. Where's the patient? Not an automobile accident, I hope? Those I dread. So sad, so unnecessary." He shouted over Dodd's shoulder. "All of you fellows out there, be quiet, do you hear me? They're good chaps," he explained to Dodd, "just a bit excitable. Now what can I do for you?"

"My name's Dodd. I'm a private detective."

"Now that's interesting, isn't it? Wait till I summon my wife. She's a great mystery fan. She's always wanted to meet a real private detective."

"I'd rather you di—"

"Oh, it's no trouble at all. We have our living quarters on the second floor. It's noisy but more convenient. You wouldn't believe the number of night emergencies I must cope with, more than any obstetrician, I'm sure. When we lived in the city I no sooner arrived home for dinner than out I would have to rush again to treat some little chap in trouble."

"The chap I came here about," Dodd said dryly, "is a Scottie."

"A fine breed. Loyal, courageous, indepen—"

"His name's Mack. He belongs to Rupert Kellogg. I talked to one of your employees about the dog earlier in the day. He said Mack was ready to be taken home."

"He *was* taken home," the doctor said with a pleased smile. "Oh, it was a joyful reunion, for both man and beast. Scotties are true Scots. They don't spend freely, they don't squander their affections on just anyone, no indeed. Fine chaps, Scotties."

"Kellogg picked the dog up himself?"

"Of course."

"When?"

"I should say between three and four o'clock. I was treating a Yorkie at the time. The poor lass has distemper, I don't think she will live. Still, we keep trying, and hoping, and, if you want the truth, praying a bit too. My wife takes care of that end of it. She's a godly woman."

"Was Kellogg alone?"

"He came in here alone. His wife waited for him out in the car."

"His wife's supposed to be in New York."

"Really? Now that's odd, isn't it? I met Mrs. Kellogg a couple of years ago when I gave Mack a rabies shot. A pretty little woman, quiet but friendly."

"And you say that the woman in the car was Mrs. Kellogg?"

"Now that you've cast some doubt on it, I can't be sure. I assumed it was Mrs. Kellogg because she was with Mr. Kellogg. Why, I even waved to her... Wait a minute. Come to think of it, she didn't wave back. There's another thing I noticed too... Mack didn't seem too anxious to get into the car. Usually, when I've had a dog here for a while, he's very eager to jump into the family car and go home."

"I have good reason to believe that Kellogg wasn't driving the family car and wasn't traveling with his own wife."

"Dear me," Dr. Sidalia said, looking uncomfortable. "He certainly doesn't give the impression of being that kind of man at all. He's very fond of animals."

"So was Dr. Crippen."

"The English murderer?"

Dodd nodded. "In fact, it was Crippen's attachment to a dog that led to his capture."

"I didn't know that. I wonder what happened to the dog after Crippen was hanged?"

"I have no idea."

"Well, I hope a good home was found for him, poor chap. It can be quite a blow to a dog, losing his master." Sidalia spoke as if the Crippen case was recent, the dog still alive, although he must have known that everyone connected with Crippen had long since died. "Why did you bring up the subject of Crippen in connection with Mr. Kellogg?"

"Kellogg's in the same kind of trouble."

"You don't mean he—murdered somebody?"

"It looks that way."

"Dear me. This is quite a shock. I must sit down."

Sidalia lowered himself into a plastic-covered chair and began fanning his face with his hand.

"The police will be here to question you," Dodd said. "Probably in an hour or two. They'll want to know about the woman and about the car."

"I never notice cars. People and animals, yes. But cars, I pay no attention to them. All I can remember is that it was dirty. I notice dirt, I'm a very meticulous man."

"Was the car new?"

"Neither new nor old. Average-looking."

"Color?"

"Greenish."

"Coupé convertible? Sedan?"

"I can't recall."

"You said that the dog didn't seem anxious to enter the car. That means you stood and watched. How did the dog get into the car?"

"Kellogg opened the door, naturally."

"Which door?"

"The rear."

"That would make the car a four-door sedan, wouldn't it?"

163

"Why, yes," Sidalia said, looking pleasantly surprised. "Yes, I believe it would."

"How did the woman react to the dog? Did she make a fuss over him? Did she reach back and pet him?"

"No. I don't think she did anything."

"Assuming that the woman was Mrs. Kellogg, would you call that normal behavior under the circumstances?"

"Dear me, no! When one of my little patients is released, there's always a good deal of excitement on the part of the family. It's one of the joys of my life, to witness these reunions."

"How was the woman dressed?"

"I only saw her head. She wore a bright red scarf tied under her chin."

"What color was her hair?"

"I can't recall that any of it was showing. She was very tanned, I know that. I remember wondering how Mrs. Kellogg could have managed a tan like that with all the fog we've had this summer. Of course, we're fairly sure now that the woman wasn't Mrs. Kellogg, so perhaps she was not tanned at all but had a naturally dark skin. These days it's hard to tell the difference, the way women bake themselves like potatoes."

Dodd thought, *a tanned or dark-skinned woman, a greenish sedan, a black dog; that's not much to go on.* "When Kellogg left, in what direction did he turn?"

"I have no idea. I went back inside as soon as he started the car. As I told you, I had a patient on the table at the time, the little Yorkie with distemper. A cruel disease, distemper, inflicted on the poor beasts usually by the carelessness of their masters. Would you care for a pamphlet on the subject of distemper immunization?"

"I don't own a dog."

"Cats also can become victims."

"I don't own a cat, either."

"Dear me, you must be a lonely man," Sidalia said with sympathy.

"I get along."

"As a matter of interest, I have two little chaps in here right now who are looking for a good home, a beautiful pair of pedigreed cocker spaniels, brothers."

"I'm afraid I…"

"You have a kind face, Mr. Dodd. I noticed, as soon as I opened the door, that you have a very kind face. I'll wager you have a way with animals."

"I live in an apartment," Dodd lied. "My landlord won't allow dogs."

"He must be an unfeeling man. I'd move out of there immediately if I were you."

"I'll think about it."

"Mark my words, a man prejudiced against animals is a man not to be trusted."

Dodd opened the door. "Thanks for the advice. And the information."

"Must you go so soon? My wife will be very disappointed at missing the chance to meet a real private detective. I'll buzz her, it won't take a minute."

"Some other time."

"Duty calls, I presume. Well, I hope I've been of some assistance. Not that I would like to get Mr. Kellogg in any trouble, he's a fine, dog-loving man."

"Whatever trouble he's in, he got there himself."

"Such is the way of the world," Sidalia said with more pity than censure. "Good-bye for now, then. And don't forget, when you move to a new place, there's no better company in the world than a pair of cocker spaniels."

"I won't forget."

Dodd realized as he got into his car that if he'd spent ten more minutes with Sidalia the back seat would now contain two cocker spaniels, and a lot of trouble. *And a lot of fun. I wonder what Doris would say if I.... No, that's crazy. One dog, maybe. But two, she'd think I'd lost my marbles. Still, not everybody is offered a pair of beautiful pedigreed cocker spaniels. By God, I bet they're cute...*

The doctor was standing on the lighted porch, waving good-bye. Dodd pressed down hard on the accelerator and the little car jumped across the driveway as if all of Sidalia's chaps were biting at its heels.

He took Portola Drive back to the city. He wasn't in any hurry. An hour ago he'd been overoptimistic about finding out what car Kellogg was driving, the make, the year, even the license plates; he had imagined himself following Kellogg, reaching him before the police did, breaking the case before they even knew there was a case.

"Dodd, boy dreamer," he said aloud. "Me and my kind face."

He was aware that the police would be waiting for him at Kellogg's house and taking a dim view of his absence, but a few more minutes wouldn't make much difference. The telephone call he intended to make had to be made in private, without Brandon or any policemen listening in.

He parked the car in front of the building where his office was located, and took the elevator up to the third floor. Lorraine, his secretary, had left a message for him in her typewriter, as she usually did when something important came up during his absence: "Spec. Del. letter from Fowler on your desk." To make sure he didn't miss the letter she had propped it between two ash trays, as if she mistrusted either his eyesight or his ability to find anything.

Dear Dodd:

Had just returned from posting my previous letter to you when Emilio called me from the Windsor bar to tell me that something *milagroso* had happened to him. I don't agree that it's miraculous, but it's interesting. Someone sent him two ten-dollar bills in an envelope postmarked San Francisco. He thought at first the money came from some lady tourist who'd taken a fancy to him. Then he remembered that O'Donnell had borrowed two hundred fifty pesos from him several months ago, roughly twenty bucks. I draw several conclusions from this:

1. O'Donnell is in S.F.
2. He has some means of support.
3. His conscience is bothering him, and he's scared. (In my experience "conscience money" usually has little to do with the debt or theft involved. It's a pay-off for other things, triggered by fear.)
4. Whatever is on his mind, it's serious enough to make him send the money anonymously, but not so serious as to make him cover his tracks completely.

These are my conclusions. Draw your own. And happy hunting!

FOWLER.

Happy hunting. Dodd repeated the words grimly, remembering the dead man on the kitchen floor. There were many mistakes in Fowler's letter: all the tenses were wrong. The hunt was over.

He picked up the phone and called a number in Atherton.

A woman answered on the second ring. "This is the Brandon residence."

"I'd like to speak to Mrs. Brandon, please."

"Mrs. Brandon has retired for the night."

"It's very important."

"She's got a headache. I have orders not to dis—"

"Is that Miss Lundquist?"

"Why, yes."

Dodd oiled up his voice. "I'm a friend of Mr. Brandon's. He's often spoken of you, Miss Lundquist."

"He has? Well, my goodness."

"My name is Dodd. I must talk to Mrs. Brandon. Tell her that, will you?"

"I guess, being as it's so important, she won't mind. Hold on."

Dodd held on, cradling the phone between his shoulder and his ear while he lit a cigarette. He could hear nothing from the other end, no whispers or sounds of movement. He thought the line was dead. Minutes passed, and he was on the point of hanging up when Helene Brandon spoke suddenly and sharply in his ear: "Hello, who is this?"

"Elmer Dodd."

"We're not acquainted."

"We are, in a sense, Mrs. Brandon. We had a telephone conversation a couple of hours ago."

"Is this your idea of a joke? I've never talked to you on the telephone or any other way."

"I was at Kellogg's house when you called. Kellogg wasn't."

After a brief pause, she said in a low, muffled voice, "Is my husband with you?"

"No."

"Does he know—about my call?"

"I haven't told him. But he's going to find out. So is everybody else in Northern California when this hits the newspapers."

"The newspapers? Why should the newspapers be interested in a private conversation between me and my brother-in-law, or what I thought was my brother-in-law? And why should you want to tell them?"

"I don't want to," Dodd said. "I have to. I've got a license to hang on to. I can't withhold evidence."

"Evidence? Of what?"

"Brandon hasn't been in touch with you?"

"No. He's not home yet. I'm beginning to worry. He's never this late, I don't know where he can be."

"He's still at Kellogg's house."

"You shouldn't have left him alone with Rupert," she said shrilly. "God knows what will happen."

"Kellogg isn't there. He's skipped town, with the police on his tail."

"Police? Why? Have they found—Amy?"

"Not Amy. A man, a stranger. He was murdered in Kellogg's house with a kitchen knife, sometime this afternoon."

"Oh, my God! Rupert—Rupert…"

"I think Kellogg meant to get rid of the body. He started to clean up the mess but there was too much of it. He decided to leave town instead. So he picked up his dog, and his girlfriend, and left."

"What girlfriend?"

"The one he lied to you about. You saw her in Lassiter's at noon." Dodd paused. "What happened, Mrs. Brandon? Did you walk in unexpectedly and louse up the rendezvous?"

She didn't answer immediately. He thought she might be crying, but when she spoke again her voice was clear and crisp, with no evidence of tears. "She came in while I was talking to Rupert at the lunch counter. She was heading straight for him until he turned and stared at her. I'm not a mind reader, but I know there was a message in that look of his. Anyway, she bought a package of cigarettes and left. When I asked Rupert about her, he said he'd never seen her before. I had a feeling then, that he was lying. I still have. But it's only a feeling, there's no evidence to back it up."

"There might be. What did the girl look like? And how much of a girl was she, and how much of a woman?"

"Early twenties. Blond, quite pretty, a bit overweight. She looked ill at ease and uncomfortable, as if her clothes were too new and too tight. I thought at the time she was a girl from the country, used to doing a lot of outside work. The tan she had wasn't the kind we get around these parts. It was more like the kind you see on the migrant workers who pick fruit and cotton on the ranches in the Valley."

"A lot of the migrants are Mexican," Dodd said.

"A lot are white too. They both end up with the same color skin."

"You said her hair was blond?"

"Bleached."

"By the sun or the bottle?"

"Even in the Valley the sun doesn't get that strong."

"Have you any reason to believe the girl came from the Valley?"

"Her feet. They were very wide and flat, as if she was used to going barefoot."

He didn't argue the point, but he knew that very few of the Valley pickers went barefoot if they could afford shoes. Under the noon sun the ground grew hot as a kiln.

"I saw her again later," Helene said. "She walked through Union Square with a man about ten years older than she was. I thought he might be her brother. He had the same coloring, and they had the same general air about them, as if they were ill at ease in the city and didn't belong there. I'm pretty sure they were arguing about something, though I didn't overhear any actual words."

"The man was wearing a plaid sport jacket?"

"Why—why, yes. How did you know?"

"I saw him."

"Were you in the Square too?"

"No. I saw him later." *The rest of a lifetime later.*

"Who is—was he?"

"An acquaintance of your sister-in-law, I think."

"You make that word 'acquaintance' sound dirty."

"Do I? Well, let's face it, Mrs. Brandon—when I dress for a job like this I don't put on clean, white gloves."

"You mean Amy and this man were…"

"Acquainted."

"It still sounds dirty."

"Maybe you're just hearing it dirty," Dodd said. "Amy and O'Donnell met in the bar of a Mexico City hotel. Amy's gone, O'Donnell's dead. Now you know as much about it as I do. For further information consult your local newspaper."

"The papers. Oh God. This will be in all the papers. Gill will…"

Dodd didn't want to be told what Gill would. He'd seen and heard enough of the man. He said brusquely, "Mrs. Brandon, when you met Kellogg at Lassiter's at noon, did he mention his wife?"

"Yes. He said Amy would be coming back soon. By Thanksgiving or Christmas."

"That's not very soon."

"Isn't it? I guess that depends on your viewpoint." She paused, as if she was trying to decide whether to tell him how she really felt about Amy. Then she said, "Do you think she's coming back?"

"I'm beginning to wonder," Dodd said, "if she ever went away."

A kitchen knife wasn't generally the kind of weapon used in a planned or premeditated murder. It was a weapon of emergency, seized upon suddenly in a moment of fury or fear. Fists were a man's customary instruments of quick attack and defense. A woman's were whatever happened to occur to her or to be handy. The knife may have been lying on the kitchen counter, ready to be picked up.

There were only five women involved in the case. One of them, Wilma Wyatt, was dead. The others were living, or presumed living: Miss Burton, Helene Brandon, the young woman with the bleached hair, and Amy herself. Of these four, only the young woman and Amy were definitely known to be acquainted with O'Donnell. But it was possible that Miss Burton had met him through Kellogg, and that even Helene Brandon, for all her protestations of innocence and ignorance, had known the dead man. Known him, and had reason to fear him. In that case, Helene's blundering phone call to Kellogg's house might not have been a blunder at all, but part of a plan with a triple purpose: to try and establish her own innocence, and to find out if the body had been discovered and identified, and to make sure that the girl with the bleached hair was brought into the case. Bringing in the girl would direct attention away from herself and her own still-obscure part in the affair.

But what possible connection, he wondered, could Helene Brandon have had with O'Donnell? And if there had been any connection, would she have freely admitted seeing O'Donnell in the Square?

No, he thought, *it doesn't make sense. The woman at the bottom of this is not Helene, it's Amy. It all comes back to Amy—where did she go and why did she leave?*

A wild idea rose to the surface of his consciousness like some improbable sea monster. Suppose Amy hadn't left at all, suppose she'd been living in that house all the time, under cover, for reasons no one yet knew. Incredible as the theory seemed, it would account for a number of things: the dismissal of the maid, Gerda Lundquist; the removal of the little dog, Mack, who might have given Amy's presence away; the letters, which had certainly been written by Amy, but not necessarily from a distance, perhaps right in her own bedroom.

Doors began opening in his mind, revealing rooms that were peopled with shadows and voiced with echoes. None of the shadows could be positively identified, and the echoes were like the nonsense syllables produced by a tape recording running backward. But in one corner of one room, a faceless woman sat at a desk, writing.

The telephone conversation with Helene Brandon continued.

"Mr. Dodd? Are you still…?"

"I'm here."

"Listen to me. Please listen. There's nothing to be gained by dragging me into this."

"You have important evidence."

"But I gave it to you. *You* have it now. That's what counts, isn't it—the evidence itself, not who tells it to the police. Can't you keep me out of it? I'll pay."

"If I keep you out of it, I'll be the one who ends up paying."

"There must be ways."

"Name one."

She was silent a moment. He could hear her heavy, irregular breathing, as if thinking was to her a violent physical exercise.

"You," she said finally, "you could have been the one who saw Rupert and the girl at Lassiter's, at lunch time."

"Maybe I could, except I ate my lunch out of a paper bag in my office."

"Alone?"

"A couple of flies joined me for dessert."

"Please, for heaven's sake, be serious. You don't know what this means to me and my family. My three children are all in school. They're old enough to suffer from this, suffer terribly."

"You can't prevent their suffering. Their uncle is wanted for murder."

"At least he's not a blood relative. I am. I'm their mother. If I'm dragged into this, God help them."

"O.K., O.K.," Dodd said flatly. "So I saw Rupert and the girl at Lassiter's. What was I doing there?"

"Having lunch."

"My secretary knows damned well I took my lunch to work."

"All right then, you were trailing Rupert—or is it tailing?"

"Either."

"When the girl came into the picture you decided to tail her instead, so you did. She went to Union Square where she met…"

"How did she get to Union Square?"

"Took the Powell Street cable car."

"Do you know that or are you making it up?"

"Making it up. But it sounds plausible, isn't that what we're aiming at? Besides, she entered the Square from Powell Street."

"What time?"

"I don't know, I sort of lost track of time. I was—thinking about Amy coming home. And other things." She coughed, as if to warn herself not to step on dangerous ground. "I remember it started to rain, and the old men who were feeding the pigeons got up and left."

"It started to rain about three o'clock." He wouldn't have

174

noticed the time or the rain particularly, except that his secretary had come into his office to tell him in her own peculiar way, that she was going down to the drugstore to buy a bottle of cold pills. *"Some people believe that rain cleanses and washes the air. But I happen to know for a fact that what it does is bring down all the viruses and bacteria from outer space, also Strontium 90. I suppose you don't care about Strontium 90, but when your bones begin to decay inside you..."*

"Three o'clock," Helene said. "Yes, it must have been about that."

"Where did she meet her friend in the plaid sport jacket?"

"I have no idea. It was simply a coincidence that I saw her again. I wasn't following her or looking for her or anything. She just appeared."

"O.K., that's how I'll have to play it, as a coincidence. The police don't like coincidences, though."

"Coincidences like that happen here all the time. In L.A. you can go downtown every day for a month and never meet a soul you've ever seen before. But here, the downtown's so small I invariably meet someone I know when I go shopping or out to lunch. It's sort of like a village in that respect."

"The natives would get restless if they heard you say that."

"It's true, though. It's one of the things I love about the city."

"All right," Dodd said. "So it was a small coincidence. I wasn't tailing the girl, she just appeared."

"Mr. Dodd, you're going to help me? You're really going to help me?"

"Not you. The kids." He wanted to, but didn't, tell her why. When he was a junior in high school, his father had been arrested on a drunk charge. It wasn't much, but it made the newspapers. He'd left school and never gone back. "Your job now, Mrs.

Brandon, is to be discreet. If the police question you, answer them. But don't volunteer any information."

"What if they find Rupert and he tells them the truth, that I was the one who saw him at Lassiter's with the girl?"

"Rupert," Dodd said, "will have a lot of other talking to do before he gets around to that."

17

When Miss Burton turned the corner it seemed to her that some-one on the street was staging a huge outdoor pageant with all the neighbors serving as members of the cast and crew. It was impossible to tell what kind of pageant it could be, the charac-ters and costumes were so varied and numerous: small boys on bicycles; women in housedresses, bathrobes, pajamas; men car-rying cameras, babies, brief cases; groups of girls twittering and chirping like birds, and grim-lipped old ladies watching in silence from the back of the stage, as if the scene they were witnessing was old, remembered stuff to them.

Both sides of the street were lined with cars, some with engines still running and the headlights on and people peering out from the open windows. Miss Burton stopped and leaned against a lamppost, feeling suddenly dizzy and breathless. *What are they trying to see?* she thought. *What do they expect to see? What are they waiting for?*

The wind clawed her hair and pinched her lips blue and tore at her yellow coat, but she was unaware of any physical suffering. People pressed past her, shouting to each other above the wind. A large white dog paused to stare at her as if she was usurping his own private lamppost.

A woman wearing a battered muskrat coat over striped paja-mas called the dog away. "He won't hurt you, he's gentle as a lamb."

"I'm not—afraid," Miss Burton said.

"You looked like you were."

"No."

"You can't see much from here, but if you go any closer you might get involved. Believe me, it doesn't pay to get involved."

"What happened?"

"Murder is what happened. In the Kelloggs' house. I've always known there was something funny about those people. Oh, they seemed nice enough, on the surface… Where are you going? Hey, wait a minute, you dropped your scarf!"

But Miss Burton was already on her way, running through the crowd, weaving in and out like a little quarterback pursued by giants.

Dodd was parking his car around the corner when he spotted her, recognizing her first by her yellow coat. She didn't see him, she would have passed by without knowing he was there if he hadn't called out to her: "Miss Burton!"

She turned to look at him, briefly and blindly, then she resumed her running. He started after her, without any plan or intention, like a dog chasing a moving object simply because it was moving. He hadn't gone fifty yards when he began to puff and a sharp pain stabbed his side. He would never have caught up with her if she hadn't stumbled over a crack in the sidewalk and fallen to her knees.

He helped her up. "Are you hurt?"

"No."

"It's a funny time to be practicing up for the four-minute mile."

"Go away. Just go away."

"What are you doing here?"

"Nothing. *Nothing.* Please leave me alone. Please."

"A lot of people are suddenly saying 'please' to me," Dodd said dryly. "I guess it takes trouble to make people talk polite."

"I'm not in trouble."

"Any friend of Kellogg's is in trouble. Have you heard from him?"

"No."

"He didn't call to say good-bye?"

"No."

"And you wouldn't tell me if he had, would you?"

"No."

"You can get away with saying no to me, but the police aren't going to like it. They're probably at your apartment right now, waiting for you. And from now on that's the way it will be. You'll be watched, followed, every place you go. If they can get to your mail before you do, they will. Your apartment will be bugged and your phone tapped."

"I have no information."

"You're loaded with information, Miss Burton. And they'll get it all. They'll take you apart like a watch, your insides will be laid out on a table. No watch ever works the same once it's been taken apart like that, unless it's done by an expert. The police aren't expert, they can be pretty damned clumsy."

As if to emphasize his point, a police car with its siren open turned the corner on two wheels. A few drivers pulled over to the curb, the rest proceeded as if they'd heard and seen nothing.

"Why," she said painfully, "why are you being so cruel?"

"Maybe, someday, you'll realize it's kindness, not cruelty, to warn you what to expect when the police start asking questions."

"I can't give out information I don't have."

"And you won't give out what you do have?"

"I told you…"

"Miss Burton, what are you doing in this neighborhood?"

At first she shook her head as if she didn't intend to answer. Then she said, slowly and carefully, "Mr. Kellogg left the office at noon. He wasn't feeling well. I decided to drop by his house and see if there was anything I could do to help."

"That's what you intend to tell the police?"

"Yes."

"They'll think you're a most solicitous and devoted secretary."

"I am."

"In fact, they might think you're more than a secretary."

"I can't help the dirt in other people's minds. Including yours."

"My mind doesn't have any dirt in it, where you're concerned."

"No?"

"No," he said firmly. "I believe you're exactly what you claim to be, a devoted secretary, with very little talent or taste for lying. Miss Burton, why were you running away when I stopped you?"

"I heard that there'd been a—a murder."

"Who told you?"

"A woman, a stranger. She said a murder had been committed in the Kellogg house."

"That's all?"

"That's all. I didn't wait to hear any more. I didn't want to get involved so I left."

"Without asking any questions?"

"Yes."

"Weren't you even curious about who was murdered?"

She turned away, silent and obstinate.

"Miss Burton, your employer was living alone, or presumably alone, in that house. Wouldn't it have been natural for you to assume that he was the one who was killed? Wouldn't it also have been natural for you to stay long enough to find out?"

Her lips moved but she didn't speak. He wondered if she was praying. He hoped so; she was going to need all the help she could get.

"Miss Burton, did you have a good reason to believe that the victim was not Rupert Kellogg?"

"No!"

"I suggest that he called you to tell you he was leaving town because something had happened. Perhaps you didn't believe him and that's why you came out here tonight, to check up on him. Or perhaps he didn't tell you exactly what had happened and you wanted to find out for yourself. Which was it?"

She put her hands over her ears. "I don't have to listen to you! I don't have to talk to you! Go away! Go away or I'll scream!"

"You are screaming," he said.

"I can scream louder."

"I'll bet you can. But you don't want to see the police any sooner than you have to, so let's play it calm, eh? You can't drown out the truth by screaming."

"What you think isn't necessarily the truth."

"Then why all the reacting? Simmer down. Do some thinking. Your story doesn't hold up. The police won't believe it any more than I do."

"I can't help..."

"You can help. Tell the truth. Do you know where Kellogg is?"

"No."

"You haven't seen him since he left the office at noon?"

"No."

"Or been in touch with him?"

"No."

"Miss Burton, a woman has disappeared and a man has been killed. Under those circumstances, withholding information is a very serious matter."

"I have no information, for you or anyone else."

"Well, I have some for you." He paused, letting her wait, giving her time to wonder, to worry. "When Kellogg left town he wasn't alone. He took his girl friend with him."

She didn't move and no expression crossed her face, but a column of color rose up from her neck to her cheek-bones and the tips of her ears. "That's a very old and very cheap trick, Mr. Dodd."

"For your sake, I wish it were a trick. But it happens to be a fact. They were seen together at noon, and again later when he picked up the dog at the kennel."

"I don't believe it. If he had a—a woman with him it must have been his wife."

"Not a chance. The girl was a pretty blonde, years younger than his wife."

"Younger." She mouthed the word as if it had an acrid taste but must be swallowed.

"Twenty-two, twenty-three."

"What's her—name?"

"If I knew, I'd tell you."

She was silent, huddling inside her yellow coat for protection, not from the wind outside but from the storm inside. She said at last, "I guess you've told me enough for tonight."

"I had to. I can't watch a woman like you jeopardize herself for a worthless man without trying to stop you."

"How do you know what kind of woman I am?"

"I do know. I knew last night when I talked to you at the dancing academy." It seemed, to Dodd, a very long time ago.

She glanced at him bitterly. "I suppose you followed me last night when I went home after class."

"You didn't go home, Miss Burton."

"So you were following me."

"No."

"Then how can you be sure where I went?"

"Kellogg told me."

"That's a lie. He doesn't know you, he's never spoken to you in his life."

"Let's say his actions spoke for him. This morning he used his power of attorney to take fifteen thousand dollars out of his wife's bank account. I deduced that someone had warned him I was on his trail. You."

He guessed from her shocked expression that it was the first time she'd heard about the money and the power of attorney. He pressed his advantage: "Did Kellogg forget to mention the fifteen thousand to you? He has a convenient memory."

"It was—the money was—is—none of my business."

"Even if he used it to skip town with a blonde? I suppose he also forgot to mention the blonde."

"You're a bad man," she said in a whisper. "A hateful man."

"If, by that, you mean you hate me, I'll have to accept it. If you mean I'm full of hate, I must correct you. I'm not full of hate. I wish you well, I'd like to help you."

"Why?"

"Because I think you're a nice girl, who's doing some wrong things with the right intentions."

"I've done nothing wrong."

"Let's say ill-advised, then." He jammed his fists into the pockets of his topcoat as if to prevent them from taking a poke at someone. "You went to Kellogg's house last night to warn him. I know that, so don't bother denying it. Now listen. This is important. You went to the front door and Kellogg let you in?"

"Yes."

"There's a long hall with several rooms off it. Did you walk down that hall?"

"Yes."

"Were the doors to those rooms open or closed?"

"Open."

"Where did you and Kellogg talk?"

"In the den, at the back of the house."

"Did you go into any of the other rooms?"

"Just what are you getting at?" she said shrilly. "Are you implying that he and I…"

"Please answer."

"I went to the bathroom. Make something of that. I went to the *bathroom*, and combed my *hair* and washed my *face* because I'd been *crying*! Now make something of it!"

He looked pained, as if the thought of her crying depressed him. "I'm not going to ask you why you were crying, Miss Burton. I don't even want to know. Just tell me one thing. Did you get the impression, while you were there, that someone else might be living in the house besides Kellogg?"

"I suppose you mean the blonde?"

"You suppose wrong. I mean Amy."

"Amy." One corner of her mouth jerked upward in a sudden little half-smile. "That's a funny idea, that's really funny." She drew in her breath and held it like a swimmer about to go underwater. "No, Amy wasn't in the house, Mr. Dodd. Not alive, anyway, not listening, not able to listen."

"How can you be sure?"

"He would never have said the things he did if anyone else had been there. Especially Amy."

So the bastard made love to her, some degree of love. Dodd found himself wondering, too hard, what degree of love. "Thank you, Miss Burton. I realize how difficult it was for you to tell…"

"Don't thank me. Just please leave me alone."

"Are you going home?"

"Yes."

"I'll drive you. My car's just down the street."

"No. No thanks. There's a bus due in five minutes."

So she even knows the bus schedule, Dodd thought. *That means she's made a lot of trips to these parts, too many.* "Well, at least let me walk you to the corner."

"I'd rather you didn't."

"All right. Go by yourself. Good night."

Neither of them moved.

He said brusquely, "Hurry up or you'll miss your bus."

"I wish I knew what side, whose side, you were on in this business."

"I was hired to find Amy. Kellogg's various extracurricular activities, like murder, theft, adultery, don't interest me except to the extent that they might lead me to Amy. Dead or alive. So you might say I'm on nobody's side. I could be on yours, but you don't want to play it that way."

"No."

"That suits me. I work better as a free agent anyway." He turned to leave. "Good night."

"Wait. Just a minute. Mr. Dodd, you can't—you can't really believe Rupert did all those things."

"I can. I'm only sorry you can't."

"I have—*faith* in him."

"Yeah. Well. That's that, isn't it?"

He wondered how long her faith would last after she'd had a talk with the police.

They were waiting for him at Kellogg's house, a sergeant whom he didn't recognize, and Inspector Ravick whom he did. Only a few hours before, the place had been, except for the dead man in the kitchen, very orderly and well kept. Now it was a shambles; the furniture had been disarranged, cigarette butts and used flash bulbs were scattered on the floors, rugs were caked with mud, and everything in the kitchen, walls and woodwork, stove, refrigerator, sink, taps, chairs, bore the black smudges of fingerprint powder.

"I see you've been making yourself at home, Inspector," Dodd said. "Is this your version of gracious living?"

A scowl crossed Ravick's broad, pock-marked face. "O.K., Weisenheim, where the hell have you been?"

"The name's Dodd. Only my best friends call me Weisenheim."

"I asked you a question."

"Well, I'm thinking of an answer."

"Make it good. Start talking."

Dodd started talking. He had a lot to say.

18

For fifty miles the road had been winding tortuously along the cliffs above the sea. In places the cliffs were so high that the sea was invisible and unheard. In other places they were low enough for Rupert to see the foam of the breakers in the light of the quarter-moon.

The little dog had begun to whimper in the back seat. Rupert spoke to him soothingly and quietly. He said nothing to his companion. They had not spoken since Carmel, and they were now passing through the Big Sur, where the redwoods stood in massive silence, disowning the wild wind and the reckless sea.

She was not asleep, although her eyes were closed and her head rested against the door. He thought, not for the first time, *what if the door should fly open on a curve, what if she fell out? That would be the end of it all. I could drive on by myself...* But he knew it wouldn't be the end, the end wasn't even in sight. He reached across her suddenly and locked the door she was leaning against.

She shrank back as if he'd aimed a blow at her head. "Why did you do that?"

"So you won't fall out." *So I won't be tempted to push you out.*

"Is it much farther?"

"We're not even halfway."

She muttered some words that he didn't understand; they might have been a prayer or a curse. Then, "I feel sick."

"Take a pill."

"All these curves, they make my stomach feel bad. There must be another road, one that is straight and smooth."

"The better roads have more cars on them. You'd feel a hell of a lot sicker if you heard a siren behind you."

"The police are not watching for this car. They don't know Joe had a car. Maybe they even don't know who he is. I took his wallet out of his pocket. That will make it harder for them." But she didn't sound very sure of it, and after a time she added, "What will we do when we get there?"

"Leave that to me."

"You promised to look after me."

"I'll look after you."

"I don't like the way you say that. Why can't we make plans, right now, right here? There is nothing else to do."

"Watch the scenery."

"We could start deciding what…"

"The deciding's done. The plans are made. You're going back."

"Back? Not—all the way back?"

"You'll take up exactly where you left off. Tell everyone you've been away on a little vacation and now you want to resume your ordinary manner of living. Act natural and don't talk too much. And remember, this isn't advice I'm giving you, it's an order."

"I am not forced to obey. I have money. I can disappear, I can get lost in the city."

"Nothing would please me more, but it won't work."

"You mean you will not let it work," she said bitterly. "You will tell."

"I'll tell. Everything I know. That's a promise."

"You don't care what happens to me, do you?"

"Not a hoot in hell. If you went up in smoke I'd just open the windows and air the car out."

"You are—you are a very changed man."

"Murder changes people."

Even above the noise of the engine he could hear the sharp intake of her breath. He turned to look at her, wishing it were for the last time. She was tugging at the red silk scarf she wore on her head as if it constricted her, prevented her from getting enough air.

He said, "Leave it on."

"Why?"

"Your hair's rather noticeable. To say the least. Keep it hidden until you can get to a beauty parlor and have it changed."

"I don't want it changed. I like it this way. I have always wanted to be…"

"Keep the scarf on."

She retied the scarf under her chin, muttering to herself and shaking her head. He thought, *she's frightened enough to take orders. That's one good sign, the only good one, she's frightened.*

For half an hour they had not met or passed another car, or seen a dwelling or any sign of human occupancy. It was as if the last people to have passed that way were the builders of the road, and that had been, Rupert judged from its condition, a long time ago. Parts of it had melted in the rain as if the concrete had been mixed with sugar. *Sugar road*, he thought grimly. *If I have a future, if I live to come this way again, that will always be its name.*

At the next bend a faint glow was visible between the massive trees, like a light at the end of a long, dark tunnel. He knew she had seen it too. She began again to complain of her stomach and her head.

"I feel sick. I want a glass of water."

"We haven't any."

"There's a light up ahead. Perhaps it is a store. You could buy some aspirin for my head and get some water."

"It would be dangerous to stop."

"I tell you, I can't go on. I feel so sick, I feel like dying."

"Go right ahead."

"Oh, you are a monster, a fiend…" The rest of the epithets were lost in a series of deep, dry retches.

He said, "Stop play acting."

She kept on retching, her body bent double, her hands against her mouth.

The glow between the trees became a neon sign identifying a group of log cabins and a dilapidated coffee shop at the Twin Trees Lodge, *reas. rates, vacancy*.

Rupert pulled off the road and braked the car. Most of the cabins were dark but lights were on in the coffee shop and a man was sitting behind the counter reading a paperback book. Either he hadn't heard the car or he was at an interesting part of the book, because he didn't look up.

In the back seat the little dog began to yelp with excitement at the forest smells and the sound of a creek running behind the cabins. Rupert told the dog to be quiet and the woman to get out of the car. Neither of them obeyed.

"You wanted to stop," he said. "All right, we stopped. Now hurry up and buy a cup of coffee or whatever you want, and we'll be on our way."

He reached across her and opened the door and she half fell out of the car, at the same time making a sudden grab for her purse. The quick, cool gesture was a tip-off that her retching hadn't been genuine. It was part of an act, though he still didn't understand its purpose. For nearly a month now she had been acting a role, speaking lines not her own, in a voice and idiom not her own. She seemed almost to have forgotten who and what she was. On only one occasion had she stepped out of the role back into herself and that was when she stood in the kitchen talking to O'Donnell. *"I'm going away"* O'Donnell had said. *"No hard feelings, eh? Don't worry, I won't talk, I don't want trouble. Just give me the money to get home again…"*

Money. The key word. He watched her as she crossed the parking lot to the coffee shop clutching her purse to her breast like a little golden monster of a baby.

He waited until she sat down at the counter before he got out of the car and closed the door as quietly as possible behind him. South of the coffee shop were the rest rooms and a public telephone booth. He headed for the booth, taking the long way around to stay out of the light of the neon sign. He knew that if he had been the one who had insisted on stopping she would have been suspicious and not let him out of her sight or hearing. As it was, she had forced the issue and so she was suspicious of nothing. She sat drinking her coffee and munching a doughnut, with the purse on the counter in front of her, where she could see it and touch it at all times.

He entered the telephone booth, put a coin in the slot and dialed long distance. It was getting late and the rush hours were over. The call went through immediately.

"Hello."

"Mr. Dodd?"

"Speaking."

"You don't know me personally, Mr. Dodd, but I have a proposition you might be interested in."

"Clean?"

"Clean enough. I know you're looking for Amy Kellogg."

"So?"

"I can tell you where she is. In return for certain services."

The man behind the counter had reheated the coffee on a little butane burner. "A bit of a warm-up, ma'am?"

191

She looked blank. "I beg your pardon?"

"That's my way of saying, how would you like another cup of coffee without paying for it?"

"Thank you."

He poured more coffee for her and some for himself. "Going far?"

"We are just traveling around seeing the country."

"Gypsying, eh? I like gypsying myself."

The word stung her ears. It meant wandering, homeless, poverty-stricken people who would steal anything. She said sharply, one hand on her purse, "We are not gypsies. Do I look like a gypsy?"

"Heck, no, I didn't mean that. I meant, like for instance you pick up and leave and you don't know where you're going."

"I know where I'm going."

"Sure. All right. Just making conversation anyway. Business is slow, not many folks around to talk to."

She realized she had made a mistake being sharp to him, he would remember her more vividly. She tried to make amends by smiling at him pleasantly. "What is the next city?"

"Highway 1 ain't long on cities. It's for scenery, finest scenery in the world. Lemme see, San Luis Obispo I guess you'd say is the next real city. When you get there you're on 101, that's the main highway."

"Is it far?"

"A good piece. If it was me, now, I'd cut across to Paso Robles from Cambria, you get to 101 faster that way."

"Is there a bus that goes by here?"

"Not often."

"But there *is* one?"

"Sure. I've been trying to arrange with the company to use my place as a lunch stop, only they say it ain't big enough and the service ain't quick enough. There's just me and the wife to handle everything."

"How many doughnuts do you have left?"

"Six, seven."

"I'll take them all."

"Sure. That'll be fifty-two cents all together with the coffee."

She opened her purse under the counter so that he couldn't see how much money she had. She wasn't sure herself, but it looked like a great deal, enough to make her free of Rupert. *If I could get away from him, if I could hide in the woods… I'm not afraid of the dark, only of the dark with him in it…*

Him. It was a curse, an epithet, a dirty word.

He was sitting behind the wheel of the car when she came out of the coffee shop. She had changed to flat-heeled shoes for comfort during the trip, and she moved with leisurely grace, not the way she moved in the city, wobbling and lurching along like a little girl wearing her mother's high heels for the first time.

Instead of coming toward the car she turned right. He thought she was going to the rest room and he settled down to wait. The clock on the dashboard clicked away the minutes as if they were merry ones. Five. Seven. Ten. At eleven, he cranked down the window of the car and called her name, as loudly as he could without attracting the attention of the man behind the counter. There was no answer.

The little dog began whimpering again, as if he realized, before Rupert did, what was happening and how to deal with it. Rupert opened the car door and the dog leaped across the back of the seat and out into the night. He circled the parking lot, nose to the ground, lifting his head at intervals to yelp in Rupert's direction. Then he turned suddenly and streaked off toward the rear of the cabins where the creek splashed down the hill to the sea.

Both the dog and the object of his chase were covered by darkness. Rupert didn't call out to either of them. He simply began following the sound of the dog's now frantic barking, walking silently among the vast trees, the noise of his footsteps muffled by layers of dense, damp redwood needles. He didn't hurry, he needed time for his eyes to adjust to the dark, and he knew the dog wouldn't stop chasing her as long as she kept running. If he had had a free choice, he would have whistled the dog to heel, put him in the car, and driven on, leaving her to wander in the woods by herself until she dropped of exhaustion. But he had no choice. She was his hope as well as his despair.

She had reached the creek and was about to cross when he caught up with her. The dog was running up and down in front of her, just out of reach of the kicks she was aiming at his head. His tail was wagging and his barking sounded more mischievous than angry, as if he thought this was a new game she was playing, throwing her foot at him instead of a tennis ball.

As Rupert approached, she began to scream strange curses at him: he was a pig, his mother was a sow, his father had horns, the little dog belonged to the devil.

He grabbed her by the wrists. "Shut up."

"No! Leave me alone!"

A light went on in one of the cabins and the silhouette of a man's head appeared at the open window. The head was cocked, listening.

Rupert said, "Someone's watching."

"I don't care!"

"You will."

194

"No!"

She struggled in his grasp. He could barely hold her; in her fury she was as strong as a man.

"If you don't behave," he said quietly, "I'll have to kill you. The water's deep enough. I'll hold your head under. You can scream all you like, then. It will just help things along."

He knew she was afraid of the water, she hated the very sight of the sea, and even the sound of water running in the shower made her nervous.

She had gone limp in his arms, as if she had already drowned of fright.

"You're going to kill me anyway," she said in a ragged whisper.

"Don't be absurd."

"I can see it in your eyes."

"Stop this nonsense."

"I can feel it in your touch. You're going to kill me, aren't you?"

Yes, I am. The words were in his mouth ready to be spoken. *Yes, I'm going to kill you. But not with my bare hands, and not now. The day after tomorrow, perhaps, or the day after that. There are things to be settled before you die.*

The beam of a flashlight flickered among the trees and a man's voice called out, "Hello out there! Hey! Ahoy!"

Rupert tightened his grip on her wrist. "You're to say nothing. I'll do the talking, understand?"

"Yes."

"And don't get any ideas about asking for help. *I'm* your help, I hope you have sense enough to realize that."

The man from the coffee shop appeared, his white apron luffing in the wind. The beam of his flashlight caught Rupert in the face like a slap.

"Say, what's going on here?"

"Sorry for the disturbance," Rupert said. "My dog jumped out of the car, and my wife and I were trying to catch him."

"Oh, is that all?" He seemed vaguely disappointed. "For a minute there I thought someone was being murdered."

Rupert laughed. It sounded genuine. "I imagine murders take place more quietly and quickly." He didn't have to imagine; O'Donnell had died almost instantly, and without a word or cry of pain. "Sorry to inconvenience you."

"Oh, that's all right. We don't get much excitement around here. I like a bit of it now and then. Keeps a person young."

"I never thought of it in that way." Rupert picked up the dog with one hand, keeping the other on his companion's wrist. There was less resistance from her than from the dog, who hated to be carried. "Well, I guess we'll be on our way. Come along, my dear. I think we've caused enough commotion for one night."

The man led the way back to the parking lot, shining his flashlight on the ground. "The wind's shifting."

"I hadn't noticed," Rupert said.

"Not many people do. But with me, it's my business to check the wind. From the way it feels now, the fog'll be rolling in pretty soon. Fog, that's our problem in these parts. When the fog comes in I might as well shut up shop and go to bed. You heading for L.A.?"

"Yes."

"If I was you, I'd cut inland as soon as I could. You can't fight fog. The best you can do is run away from it."

"Thanks for the advice. I'll bear it in mind." Rupert thought, *there are lots of things beside fog that you can't fight, that you have to run away from.* "Good night. Perhaps we'll be seeing you again."

"I'll be here. Got all my money tied up in the place, can't afford to go away." He laughed sourly, as if he'd played a bad joke on himself. "Well, good night, folks."

When he had gone, Rupert said, "Get in the car."

"I don't want…"

"And hurry up. You've already delayed us half an hour with your histrionics. Do you realize how far news can travel in half an hour?"

"The police will be looking for you, not me."

"Whichever one of us they're looking for, if they find us they'll find us both together. Understand that? Together. Till death do us part."

19

Señor Escamillo yanked open the door of the broom closet and found Consuela with one ear pressed against her listening wall.

"Aha!" he cried, pointing a fat little forefinger at her. "So, Consuela Gonzales is up to her old tricks again."

"No, señor. I swear on my mother's body…"

"You could swear on your father's horns and I do not believe you. If I were not so desperate for experienced help I would never have begged you to come back." He thought briefly of the real reason he'd asked her to come back; perhaps he'd been a fool to lend his services to such a wild, American scheme. He consulted his big, gold pocket watch, which didn't keep good time but served as a useful prop to hold his staff in line. "It is now seven o'clock. Why are you not placing fresh towels in the rooms and turning down the beds?"

"I have already attended to most of the rooms."

"And why not all of them, pray? Are the towels so heavy, such a burden, that you must stop to rest every five minutes?"

"No, señor."

"I wait for the explanation," Escamillo said, with cold dignity.

Consuela looked down at her feet, wide and flat in their straw *espadrilles. Clothes*, she thought, *it's clothes that make the difference. Here I am dressed like a peasant, so he treats me like a peasant. If I had on my high heels and my black dress and my necklaces, he would be polite and call me señorita, he wouldn't dare to say my father had horns.*

"I wait, Consuela Gonzales."

"I have attended to all the rooms except 404. I was prepared to do that one too, but when I stopped at the door I heard noises from inside."

"Noises? How so?"

"People were arguing. I thought it would be wiser if I didn't disturb them, if I waited until they went out for the evening."

"People were arguing in 404?"

"Yes. Americans. Two American ladies."

"You swear it on your mother's body?"

"I do, señor."

"Oh, what a liar you are, Consuela Gonzales." Escamillo put his hand over his heart to show how much the situation pained him. "Or else you have lost your judgment."

"I heard them, I tell you."

"You tell me, yes. Now *I* tell *you*. The suite 404 is empty. It has been empty for nearly a week."

"That can't be. I heard, with my own ears…"

"Then you need new ears. Four hundred four is empty. I am the manager of this establishment. Who would know better than I which rooms are occupied and which are not?"

"Perhaps, while you were away from the desk for a few minutes, someone checked in, two American ladies."

"Impossible."

"I know what I hear." Consuela's cheeks were the color of red wine as if the blood in her veins had fermented with fury.

"This is bad," Escamillo said, "to hear things other people do not."

"You haven't tried. If you would place your ear here, at the wall…"

"Very well. The ear is here. And now?"

"Listen."

"I am listening."

"They are moving around," Consuela said. "One of them is wearing many bracelets, you can hear them clanking. There. Now they are talking. Do you hear voices?"

"Certainly I hear voices." Escamillo stepped briskly out of the broom closet, brushing lint off the sleeves and lapels of his suit. "I hear your voice and my voice. From an empty room I hear nothing, praise Jesus."

"The room is not empty, I tell you."

"And I tell you once again, stop this nonsense, Consuela Gonzales. I think you have not been saying your beads often enough lately and God is angry with you, making noises that you alone can hear."

"I have done nothing to make Him angry with me."

"We are all sinners." But Escamillo's tone implied strongly that Consuela Gonzales was the worst of the lot and she was to expect only a minimum of mercy, if any. "You had better go down to the bar and ask Emilio for one of those new American pills that ease the mind."

"There is nothing the matter with my mind."

"Is there not? Well, I am too busy to argue."

She leaned against the door of the broom closet and watched Escamillo disappear into the elevator. Globules of sweat and oil stood out on her forehead and upper lip. She brushed them off with a corner of her apron, thinking, *he is trying to frighten me, embarrass me, make me out a fool. I will not be made out a fool. It is easy to prove the room is occupied. I have a key. I will unlock the door, very quietly, and open it, very suddenly, and there they will be, arguing, moving around. Two ladies. Americans.*

Her ring of keys, suspended from a rope belt around her waist, struck her thigh and tinkled like coins as she moved toward 404.

She hesitated at the door, hearing nothing now but the traffic from the *avenida* below and the quick rhythmical drumming of her own heart.

Only a month ago, two American ladies had occupied this very room. They too had argued. One of them wore many bracelets and a red silk suit, and painted her eyelids gold. And the other…

But I must not think of those two. One is dead, the other is far away. I am alive and here.

From her key ring she chose the key labeled *apartamientos* and inserted it quietly into the lock. A quick turn of the key to the left and of the doorknob to the right and the door would open to reveal the occupants of the room and Escamillo would be proved the cowardly liar that he was.

The key would not turn. She tried one hand and then the other, and finally both together. She was a strong woman, used to heavy work, but the key wouldn't budge.

She rapped sharply on the door and called out, "This is the chambermaid. I must change the towels. Please let me in. I have lost my key. Please open the door? Please?"

She caught her lower lip with her teeth to stop its trembling. *The room is empty,* she thought. *Escamillo is right, God is punishing me. I hear voices no one else can hear, I talk to people who are not there, I listen at walls that say nothing.*

She hesitated only long enough to cross herself. Then she turned and ran down the corridor to the service stairway. In flight, she tried to pray. Her mouth moved but no words came out, and she knew it was because she had not said her beads for a long time; she could not even remember where she had put them.

Four flights down, and she was in the little room behind the bar where Emilio and his assistants came to sneak cigarettes and finish off the dregs of bottles and count the day's tips.

She had made so much noise crashing down the steps that Emilio himself hurried back to see what the fuss was about.

"Oh, it's you." Emilio was bold and elegant in a new red bolero trimmed with silver buttons and orange braid. "I thought it was another earthquake. What do you want?"

She sat down on an empty beer case and held her head in her hands.

"How's Joe?" Emilio said.

The American was waiting in Escamillo's office, pacing up and down as if he couldn't find a door to escape through. He looked worried, as worried as Escamillo felt. Escamillo, from the beginning, had had grave doubts about the situation, but Mr. Dodd was very persuasive. He'd made the plan sound both reasonable and practicable.

Escamillo was afraid it was neither, although so far he hadn't indicated his misgivings. He said simply, "Everything is in readiness. They are arguing very well together, very real."

"And Consuela is listening?"

"Certainly. Listening, it is a long habit with her."

"Did you have the lock changed?"

"Just as I was instructed, so everything has been performed. She can gain access to the room only when the ladies are ready to receive her. Also, the silver box—I gave it to Emilio as you told me to do. However, I do not understand about the silver box. Why was it necessary to purchase an exact duplicate? I begin to wonder." Escamillo's face, normally as bland as a marshmallow, was contorted in anticipation of disaster. "I begin to have doubts."

"That makes two of us."

"Señor?"

"We all have doubts," Dodd said flatly. "Let's just hope hers are bigger."

"She is not a fool, you know. A cheat, a liar, a thief, all those, but not a fool."

"She's superstitious and she's scared."

"*She* is scared, ha! And who is not? I feel my liver turning cold and white like snow."

"There's nothing to be scared of. Your part in this is finished."

"I must remind you that this is *my* hotel, *my* reputation is at stake, *I* am responsible for..." The telephone on Escamillo's desk began to ring. He darted across the room and picked it up. His small pudgy hands were quivering. "Yes? That is good, very good." He put the phone down and said to Dodd, "It has worked so far. She is with Emilio. He is very clever, you can trust him."

"I have to."

"Señor Kellogg will be here soon?"

"He's waiting in the lobby now."

"Suppose there is violence? Violence distresses me." Escamillo pressed his hand against his stomach. "You have not taken me entirely into your confidence, señor. A little voice keeps telling me that there is something questionable about all this, perhaps even something illegal."

A little voice kept telling Dodd the same thing but he couldn't afford to listen.

"How is Joe?" Emilio repeated.

"Joe?" She raised her head and stared at him blankly. For a moment the blankness was genuine—Joe was long ago and far away and dead. "Joe who?"

"You know Joe who."

"Oh, him. I haven't seen him. He was no good. He ran off with another woman."

"An American?"

"Why do you say that?"

"He sent me 250 pesos that he owed me. It was marked on the envelope, San Francisco."

"Ah, so? Well, I hope she is very rich so he will be very happy."

There'd been two rich ladies, Consuela thought. *They were ready to be plucked like chickens, but all Joe got out of it was a second-hand car and a few clothes to be buried in, because he lost his nerve, he began feeling sorry for people. His mind had turned soft as his belly.*

No, no, I must not think of that, of the blood...

"What happens with you?" Emilio said. "You look bad, like a ghost."

"I have a—a headache."

"Perhaps you would like a bottle of beer?"

"Yes. Thank you. Thank you very much."

"Do not thank me so hard," Emilio said dryly. "I expect you to pay."

"I will pay. I have money."

She thought, *I have money I can't spend, clothes I can't wear; I have bottles of perfume, yet I must go around smelling like a goat. You would steal the smell off a goat*, Joe had said.

It seemed funny to her now. She began to laugh softly, cupping her mouth in her hands so that no one would hear her and want to know why she was laughing. It would be too hard to explain; she wasn't quite sure of the reason herself.

Emilio returned carrying a bottle of cheap beer. He gave her the beer, then held out his hand for the money. She put a peso in it, grudgingly, as if it were her last.

"This," he said, "is not enough."

"It is all I have."

"I hear different. I hear you had a winning ticket last week."

"No."

"This is what I hear, that you took all your money and hid it away. If this is so…"

"And it is not."

"But suppose it is. Then you are in luck, because I have a fine bargain for you."

"I have seen too many of your fine bargains."

"Not like this." From one of the higher shelves behind the door Emilio took an object wrapped in a copy of *Grafico*. He removed the newspaper and held out, for her to see, a box of hammered silver. "A beauty, is it not?"

She pressed the cold bottle against her burning forehead like a poultice.

"As you can see," Emilio said, "it has a damage, a dent. That is why I am offering it at the absurd price of two hundred pesos. Go on, take it, feel its weight. It's genuine silver, as heavy as a mourner's heart, and what could be heavier than that, eh, Consuela?"

"Where," she said, "where did you get it?"

"Ah, that is my little secret."

"You must tell me. I must know."

"Very well. I found it."

"Where?"

"A lady left it behind in the bar, on one of the seats."

"What lady?"

"If I knew the lady I would return the box," he said severely. "I am an honest man, I would never keep what belongs to another, never. But," he added with a shrug, "since I do not know the lady's name, and since she looked very rich, with many gold bracelets, yes, even gold on her eyelids…"

*

205

The telephone rang in 404. Both the women jumped, as if they'd heard a shot. Then the one in the red silk suit crossed the room and picked up the telephone. "Yes?"

"She'll be back up soon," Dodd said. "Leave the door partly open so she can get in. Is Mrs. Kellogg all right?"

"Yes."

"And you?"

"I'm nervous. I feel so grotesque in this getup, with all this paint on. I don't know if I can go through with it."

"You have to, Pat."

"But I'm not an actress. How can I fool her?"

"Because she's ready to be fooled. The others have done their part—Escamillo, Emilio. Now it's your turn. Kellogg will be there shortly. So will I. I'll be in the other room, so don't worry."

"All right," Miss Burton said. "All right." She put down the telephone and looked across the room at the woman sitting on the edge of one of the twin beds. "She's coming up soon. We must be ready."

"Oh God," Amy whispered. "I'm not sure. Even now, I'm not *sure*."

"Everyone else is. All of us. We're sure."

"How can you be, if I'm not?"

"Because we know you and your character. We know you couldn't possibly…"

"But I tell you, sometimes I remember, I remember quite clearly. I picked up the silver box, I was going to throw it over the balcony as Wilma had challenged me to do. She tried to grab the box from me, and we struggled, and then I hit…"

"You can't remember what didn't happen," Miss Burton said sturdily.

*

206

"…and a beautiful silk suit," Emilio said, "the color of blood. My most favorite color. Your most favorite too, Consuela?"

She didn't hear the question. She was staring at the silver box as if it contained all the imps of hell. "The woman who left it, you said you'd never seen her before?"

"Wrong. I told you I did not know her name. Of course I have seen her before. She and her friend, one night in the bar they had a long talk with Joe, very gay, very merry, lots of *tequila*."

"No. I don't believe you. It's not possible."

"Ask Joe," Emilio said, "next time you see him."

"I won't be—seeing him."

"Ah, you might be surprised. One of these days you might open a door, expecting nothing, and there he'll be…"

"No, that is imposs—"

"There he'll be, the same as ever, as good as new." Emilio was grinning nervously. "And he'll say, 'Here I am, Consuela, I have come back to you and your warm bed and I will never leave you again. Always I will be at your side, you will never get rid of me.'"

"Quiet," she screamed. "Pig. Liar." She was holding the bottle of beer by the neck as if she intended to use it to silence him. The beer gurgled out on the wooden floor and through the cracks, leaving a trail of bubbles. "He will never come back."

Emilio's grin had disappeared and a white line of fear circled his dry mouth. "Very well. He will never come back. I do not argue with a lady with so many muscles and a bad temper."

"The box—the woman—it's all a trick."

"How do you mean this, a trick? I do not play tricks."

"Señor Kellogg gave you that box. And there is no such woman as you claim."

Emilio looked genuinely puzzled. "I know no Señor Kellogg. As for the woman, well, I saw what I saw. My eyes are not liars.

207

She and her little brown-haired friend came in about 5:30. I served them myself. I said, 'Good afternoon, señoras, it is a great pleasure to see you once more. Have you been away?' And the señora in the blood-colored suit said, 'Yes, I have been away on a long, long journey. I never thought I would get back, but here I am, here I am again.'"

"My beads," she said, and the beer bottle dropped from her hand and rolled, unbroken, across the wooden floor. "I must find my beads. The closet—perhaps I left them in the closet. I must go and find them. My beads... Hail Mary, full of Grace..."

Rupert and Dodd waited in the bedroom.

"A devil on the one hand," Rupert said, "and a delusion on the other. And I was trapped between them. I could do nothing but stall for time, keep Amy hidden away until she was able to think clearly again, to distinguish between what had happened and what Consuela claimed had happened. I had to keep her hidden not only from the police but from her family or anyone else she might try to 'confess' to. I couldn't afford the risk of somebody believing her confession. There were times I almost believed it myself, it was so sincere and so plausible. But I knew my wife, I knew her to be incapable of violence against another human being.

"Consuela's lies started the delusion, but it was aggravated by Amy's own feeling of worthlessness. All her life she had suffered from a nameless guilt. Now Consuela had given it a name, murder. And Amy accepted it, because it is sometimes easier to accept one specific thing, no matter how bad, than to go on living with a lot of obscure and indefinite fears. But there were other reasons too for her acceptance. She was beginning to feel hostility toward Wilma and to resent Wilma's domination. These feelings were later translated into guilt. Also, remember that Amy was drunk, and consequently had no clear recollection of the facts to counteract Consuela's false version of them."

"You claim it's false," Dodd interrupted. "But are you sure?"

"If I weren't sure, would I have confided in you and put myself at your mercy? Would I have brought you and Amy down here, dragged Miss Burton into this, broken any number of laws? Believe me, Mr. Dodd, I'm sure. It's Amy who isn't. That's why we're here now. We can't let her spend the rest of her life thinking that she killed her best friend. She didn't. I know that, I knew it from the first."

"Then why didn't you give Consuela a quick, firm brushoff?"

"I couldn't. By the time I reached Amy at the hospital, the damage had already been done. Amy was convinced she was guilty and Consuela stuck to her story. If it had been a simple matter of dealing with the girl alone, there would have been no problem. But there was Amy too. And on my side, I had no evidence at all, only my knowledge of my wife's character. Bear in mind, also, that we were in a foreign country. I was completely ignorant of police procedure, of what the authorities might do to Amy if they believed her confession."

When Rupert paused for breath, Dodd could hear the two women in the adjoining room talking, Amy softly, nervously, Miss Burton with brisk assurance, as if by putting on Wilma's clothes and make-up she had assumed some of Wilma's mannerisms. The stage was set but the leading character had yet to appear. *The silver box should do it*, he thought. *She's got to come back up to check Emilio's story about the two Americans.*

"I had no choice," Rupert continued, "but to yield to Consuela's demands and to stall for time. I talked it over with Amy and she agreed to do what I suggested, stay out of sight for a while. We got off the plane at L.A. and I checked her into a rest home under a different name, without even her own clothes to identify her."

"That's why you let the luggage go through to San Francisco?"

"The luggage and Consuela," he added grimly. "She was sitting across the aisle from us. I was able to get official papers for her by pretending I was hiring her as a nurse-companion for my wife."

"Didn't Mrs. Kellogg object to the idea of entering a rest home?"

"No, she was quite docile about it. She trusted me and knew I was trying to help her. I felt reasonably certain that in a rest home, no matter what story she told, no one would believe her. As it turned out, she kept her secret to herself. And she obeyed my orders, gave me her power of attorney before we left Mexico City, wrote the letters I dictated in order to forestall any suspicions on the part of her brother Gill. I arranged with a business associate to have one of the letters postmarked New York but Gill wasn't taken in. I didn't realize how strong his suspicions would be or the extent of his dislike for me.

"As soon as I did realize, thanks to Helene, I began to get rattled and make mistakes. Big mistakes, like leaving Mack's leash in the kitchen and giving Gerda Lundquist a chance to catch me in that fake telephone call. It seemed that with each mistake I made, the next one became easier. I could no longer think clearly, I was so worried about my wife. I had relied heavily on the theory that the passage of time would bring Amy to her senses. I was too optimistic. Time alone couldn't do the trick; something more positive was needed. But I could do nothing positive, not even go down to Los Angeles to see her, to reason with her. I was trapped in San Francisco, with you and Gill Brandon on my tail. It was, ironically, Consuela herself who forced me to do something positive."

*

210

They'd met, by prearrangement, in the back row of loges of a movie theater on Market Street. Rupert arrived first and waited for her. When she finally arrived, she had doused herself so extravagantly with perfume that before he saw or heard her approach he could smell her as she walked up the carpeted steps.

It was not the time or place for amenities, even if she'd known or cared about them. She said bluntly, "I need more money."

"I haven't any."

"Get some."

"How much were you thinking of?"

"Oh, a lot. There are two of us now."

"Two?"

"Joe and I, we got married yesterday. I have always wanted to get married."

"For God's sake," Rupert said. "Why did you have to drag O'Donnell into this?"

"I dragged no one. I simply wrote him a letter because I was lonesome. You do not understand how it is, being without friends, seeing only people who hate you and wish you dead. So I wrote Joe a letter, telling him how well I was doing, and about my pretty clothes and jewelry and my new hair, more blond than his even. I think it made him jealous. Anyway he borrowed some money and came up here by bus. Seeing him again, I thought, well, now that he's here we might as well get married and regain the blessing of the Church. So now there are two of us."

"To be supported by me."

"Not you. Your wife. You have done nothing to be ashamed of. Why should you pay? It is Mrs. Kellogg who must pay."

"This is blackmail."

"I do not concern myself with words, only money."

"You've told O'Donnell everything, I suppose?"

"We are man and wife," she said virtuously. "A wife must confide in her husband completely."

"You're a damned fool."

He felt her stiffen in the seat beside him. "Not such a fool as you might think."

"Do you realize the penalty for blackmail?"

"I realize that you cannot go to the police and complain against me. If you do, they will have to question Mrs. Kellogg and she will admit her guilt."

"That's where you're wrong," he said quickly. "My wife no longer believes your story about Mrs. Wyatt's death. She remembers the truth."

"What a bad liar you are. I can always tell a bad liar, I being such a good one."

"Yes, I know that well."

"Only I do not lie about vital matters, like Mrs. Wyatt's death."

"Don't you?"

"Must I keep telling you? I was in the broom closet, sleeping, and I woke up when I heard someone screaming in 404. I rushed in. The two women were struggling over the silver box—they'd been arguing about it when I was in the room before. As I approached, Mrs. Kellogg got hold of the box and struck Mrs. Wyatt on the head. The balcony doors were open. Under the force of the blow, Mrs. Wyatt stumbled backwards out on to the balcony and fell over the railing. My mind is very quick. I thought immediately, what a terrible thing if the police accuse Mrs. Kellogg of murder. So I picked up the box and threw it over the railing. Mrs. Kellogg had fainted from shock. I poured some whiskey down her throat from the bottle on the bureau, and when she came to a little, I said to her, 'Don't worry. I am your friend. I will help you.'"

Friend. Help. Rupert stared in silence at the oversized movie screen where a man was stalking a woman, intent on killing her. He had a brief, childish wish that he were the man and Consuela the woman. If Consuela died, naturally, or by accident, or by design...

No, he thought. It would solve nothing. I must try to save Amy, not to punish Consuela. With Consuela dead I would have no chance of proving to Amy that she is suffering from a delusion. I must keep the devil alive because without her I cannot kill the delusion.

"The sea and the fog," Consuela was saying. "They do not agree with my health. I want to go back home where it is high and dry. But of course I will require money."

"How much?"

"Fifteen thousand dollars."

"You must be crazy."

"Oh, I know it sounds like a great deal, but once you have paid, you will be rid of me. Is it not worth that much to be rid of me?" She added softly, "Joe is not stupid. He has investigated. He has found out about the piece of paper you have that lets you cash checks on your wife's account."

"A check that large is bound to attract attention."

"You have already attracted much attention. A little more won't matter. You will get the money?"

"I guess I have to."

"Very well. Tomorrow, at noon, I'll come to the restaurant where you eat lunch, Lassiter's. I'll sit down beside you, as if by accident, and when you give me the money, that will be the end of the whole thing."

"Why meet at such a public place as a restaurant?"

"Simply because it is a public place. With so many people around, you won't change your mind and try to do something foolish. I am not afraid of you, but then I can't trust you either; you love that little wife of yours too desperately. How does it happen, such a love as this?"

"That's something," he said grimly, "you'll never find out."

They missed contact at Lassiter's because of Helene's surprise appearance. Rupert went home, and later in the afternoon...

"...About 3:30," Rupert continued, to Dodd, "they drove up to the house in a second-hand car O'Donnell had bought with some of the money I'd already paid Consuela. They came around to the back door and I let them into the kitchen. They'd obviously been quarreling. Consuela was in a temper and O'Donnell seemed very nervous and frightened. I think he'd begun to realize that he had a tiger by the tail and the only thing he could do was to let go, run like hell, and hope for the best. O'Donnell's mistake was in announcing his intention of letting go. It gave the tiger a chance to prepare to spring.

"As soon as I handed the money over to Consuela, O'Donnell told her he wanted out, that he didn't intend to go with her back to Mexico City or any other place. I got the impression that they often had violent quarrels and that this one was no different. I went into the den. I could hear her screaming about marriage vows and the blessing of the Church. Then he said something to her in Spanish, and everything suddenly became very quiet. When I went back into the kitchen O'Donnell was lying in front of the refrigerator, dead, and Consuela was standing with the knife in her hand, looking surprised.

"The whole thing was so quick, so incredible, that it seemed to be taking place in a dream. I was too stunned to think clearly or to make plans. I could only act, automatically, by instinct. I tried to clean up the mess with bath towels, but it was no use, there was too much of it. Consuela kept crying and moaning, partly in regret over what she'd done, but more, I think, in dismay over what was going to happen to her now. It was at this point that I realized I had accepted too passive a role in the whole business. If

I was to help Amy, I had to do something more positive. I couldn't just sit back and wait for time to restore her to her senses. And so it was, as I said, Consuela herself who forced me to action by her killing of O'Donnell.

"Armchair critics, and people who've never been in my position, may censure me for not immediately calling the police. But you know, Dodd, that I couldn't afford to; that if I had, my wife might very well be in jail right now. Consuela would have told the authorities her story of Wilma's death, and Amy, ten chances to one, would have confirmed it. So in order to protect my wife, I had also to protect Consuela. For a time, anyway.

"We started out, using O'Donnell's car for obvious reasons. When I stopped at the kennel to get Mack, I had some wild notion of ditching Consuela, picking up Amy at the rest home, and just taking off with her and Mack and disappearing. But I knew this wouldn't work out, that in some way I must get Amy and Consuela to confront each other. I figured that Amy was a little more sure of herself by this time, and Consuela a great deal less. From such a meeting I hoped the truth would emerge. That's why I called you from the Big Sur, and asked your help in arranging it. I'm aware that I've put you in a very difficult position, but believe me, it's for a good cause. My wife's whole future is at stake."

So is mine, Dodd thought, and started making a mental list of the number of laws he'd broken in the interests of Amy's future. He stopped at seven; the project was too depressing.

In the adjoining room the telephone began to ring and Dodd went to answer it. The two women watched in silence as he picked up the phone. "Yes?"

"I sent Pedro up with the silver box," Escamillo said. "Did you receive it?"

"Yes."

"Emilio is now in my office. He tells me she is on her way upstairs."

"Thanks." Dodd replaced the phone and turned to Amy, who was sitting on the edge of the bed looking pale and bewildered, as if she'd somehow wandered into the whole affair by mistake. "Are you ready, Mrs. Kellogg?"

"I guess I am."

"How do you feel?"

"All right. I guess all right." Her hands plucked listlessly at one of the chenille roses of the bedspread. "I wish Rupert were here."

"He's right in the next room."

"I wish he were here."

Exasperation showed in his face and posture. "Mrs. Kellogg, I needn't remind you that a lot of people have gone through a great deal for your sake, especially your husband."

"I know. I know that."

"You've got to cooperate."

"I will."

"Of course she will," Miss Burton said in a hearty voice, but her bracelets clanged nervously and one of her golden eyelids twitched in dissent.

When Dodd had left, Amy sat on the bed repeating his words to herself: *A lot of people have gone through a great deal for my sake. Especially Rupert. I've got to cooperate. Because a lot of people have gone through a great deal for my sake I've got to cooperate—got to...*

As soon as Consuela opened the door of her broom closet she could hear the voices again. They were indistinct, until she pressed her ear to the listening wall, and then she heard, quite clearly, the sound of her own name, Consuela. And again, Consuela, as if they were calling her, summoning her.

No, she thought, *no, that is impossible. Escamillo said the suite was empty, and I went to the door myself, and knocked, and no one answered. The voices are heard by me alone. Perhaps I have a fever. That must be it, of course. In a fever the mind often plays tricks; one imagines, one sees and hears things that are not so.*

She raised one hand and touched her forehead. It felt moist and cool, like a newly peeled peach. No trace of a fever. *Still, it must be there,* she thought. *So far it is all on the inside and hasn't yet come to the surface. I must go home and take precautions against the evil eye that someone has cast upon me.*

But when she stepped out into the corridor she saw that the door of 404 was partly open. She knew it could not have been blown open by the wind—half an hour ago it had been so securely fastened that her passkey wouldn't budge in the lock.

She crept along the wall to the half-open door and peered inside. There were two women in the room. One of them, the small brown-haired one sitting on the bed, was alive. The other, standing in front of the open balcony door, had died almost a month ago. Consuela had seen her die from this very doorway, had heard her final scream. Now she had stepped from her coffin, groomed and jeweled as if she'd been to a party, wearing the same red silk suit and the same fur coat, untouched by any worms or mildew or decay. A month of death hadn't changed her at all; even her expression, when she saw Consuela, was the same, annoyed and impatient.

"Oh, it's you," she said. "Again. Every time I take a breath around this place someone comes creeping in to change the towels or turn down the beds. I feel as if I'm being spied on."

"They just try to give us good service," her companion said.

"Good service? The towels all stink."

"I hadn't noticed."

"You smoke too much. Your sense of smell isn't as sharp as mine. They stink."

"I don't think you should talk like this in front of the girl."

"You can tell from her face she doesn't understand a word I'm saying."

"But the travel agency said everyone on the hotel staff spoke English."

"All right, why don't you try her out?"

"I will," Amy said. "What's your name, girl? Do you speak English? Tell us your name."

Consuela stood, mute as a stone, her right hand clutching the little gold cross she wore around her neck, her eyes fixed on the hammered silver box lying on the coffee table. *It has all happened before*, she thought, *and it will all happen again. It is not that the American lady died and has come back from her grave. It is that we are all dead, all three of us, dead and in hell. This is what hell is, everything goes on repeating and repeating, forever and ever, and nobody can change it. The whole thing has happened before, and it will happen again. Pretty soon they will start to quarrel about the silver box, they will struggle over it. And I will stand here and watch her die, and listen to her last scream...*

"No! No! Please! No!" She fell forward on her knees, pressing the little gold cross against her dry lips, mumbling in Spanish the words of her childhood: "Holy Mary, Mother of God, pray for us sinners, now and at the hour of our death."

She went on praying, only partly aware of other people rushing into the room, of men's voices shouting at her, asking her questions, calling her names.

"Liar."

"You must tell us the truth."

"What happened to Mrs. Wyatt?"

"You killed her yourself, didn't you?"

"You came into this room and found Mrs. Kellogg unconscious, and Mrs. Wyatt too drunk to defend herself. And you saw your big chance."

"You must tell us the truth."

She began again, for the fifth time, "Hail Mary, full of Grace. Blessed art thou amongst women..." But the words were automatic and had no connection with her thoughts: *I am in hell. This is another corner of it, when you tell the truth and no one believes you because you have lied in the past. So you must lie to be believed.*

"Consuela, do you hear me? You must give us the truth."

She raised her head. She looked stunned, as if someone had struck a blow in a vital place, but her voice was quite clear. "I hear you."

"What happened when you came into this room?"

"She was standing on the balcony with the silver box in her hands. She leaned over the railing and disappeared. I heard her scream."

"And Mrs. Kellogg had nothing to do with it?"

"Nothing." She kissed the little cross. "Nothing."

20

"Amy, dear." It was almost midnight. The others had gone, and Rupert was alone with his wife. "You mustn't cry any more. It's all over. Tomorrow we'll go home, we'll both try to forget this past month."

She stirred in his arms like a fretful child kept up long past her bedtime. "I can never forget."

"Not entirely, perhaps. But it will become dimmer for you, more bearable."

"You're very kind to me."

"Nonsense."

"I wish I could repay you."

"You already have," he said gently. "By remembering the truth. By getting back your confidence and your belief in yourself."

"Your confidence in me was never shaken?"

"Never."

"That's because you love me."

"Partly. It's also because I know you, I know you better than you know yourself."

"Do you?" She stirred again and sighed. "You've been through so much for my sake, haven't you, Rupert?"

"Oh, not so much."

"What if I'm not worth it?"

"There you go again. Stop talking like that. It hurts me."

"Why?"

"Because I love you."

"I love you too, Rupert." She lay against her husband's heart, listening to its familiar beat, and to the noises of the alien city.

A lot of people have been through a great deal for my sake, especially Rupert. I've got to cooperate…

They were at the airport when the plane landed, Gill looking flushed and a little sheepish, and Helene wearing a big, cheerful smile as real as the plastic carnation she had pinned to her lapel.

"Darlings!" Helene shrieked, and put her arms around them both. "How wonderful to see you! Did you have a nice flight? You're both looking simply tremendous. I've got a million questions to ask, but I promise to be good and not ask a one until we get in the car. Gill, dear, why don't you go and claim their luggage?"

"I'll go with you, Gilly," Amy said. "We have so much to talk about."

"Yes. Yes, we have." Gill took her arm and began guiding her through the crowd toward the baggage department. "You're looking well."

"Oh, I feel fine."

"I guess I have a lot of apologies to make to Rupert."

"That won't be necessary. He understands. He's a very understanding man. In some ways."

Gill glanced down at her, a little puzzled by her tone. "In some ways?"

"Well, I mean, he doesn't understand everything. The way you do."

"But I don't. I've never claimed…"

"I mean, about me. He doesn't understand about me, the way you do. You see, he loves me, it's given him a blind spot. With you it's different. I've never been able to keep anything from you. Somehow or other, you've always found out."

"Not always."

"Rupert's a marvelous man, Gilly. When I think of all he's been through for my sake, all he's suffered…" She hesitated, her hand on his arm, as light as a bird. "You mustn't ever tell him, Gilly. It would make him feel so bad."

He felt the bird on his arm growing, becoming heavier. "I don't know what you mean, Amy."

"It will be one of our secrets, the biggest one. You must never tell anyone else at all, especially Rupert."

"Tell him what?"

"That I killed Wilma."

**ALSO AVAILABLE
FROM MARGARET MILLAR**

MARGARET
MILLAR

PUSHKIN VERTIGO

"A genius of plot twists" *LA Review of Books*

A classic psychological thriller

*A Stranger
in My Grave*

"The master of the surprise ending" *Independent*